ALSO BY TINA FOLSOM

LAWFUL WIFE

ETERNAL BACHELORS CLUB #3

TINA FOLSOM

Dear Cynthia!

Enjoy Bookcon!

Tina Folsom

Cover design: Tina Folsom
Cover photo: bigstockphoto.com
Author Photo: © Marti Corn Photography

Printed in the United States of America

1

Daniel rolled over and draped his arm across Sabrina's waist, pulling her closer so her back was to his front. His morning hard-on pressed against her soft, warm backside, jerking in anticipation. God, he was hungry for her. How could he not be? She was so pliant and voluptuous.

It was moments like these—waking up with Sabrina in his arms—that made him wonder how he'd gotten so fortunate as to find her. Even in the mornings, with her long dark hair a mess, she looked gorgeous. Every day she grew more beautiful. The first time he'd laid eyes on her and gazed into her green eyes, he'd known that he had to have her. That she was actually here now, in his arms, in his bed, was a miracle in itself after all the bumps that had littered their road to happiness. But they'd overcome those obstacles. Now nothing could go wrong anymore. In a few days, Sabrina would be his wife.

Sabrina moaned softly and wiggled closer to him, her behind rubbing on his painfully hard cock. He lowered his lips to her shoulder and pressed small kisses on her warm skin, while nudging his cock between her thighs.

"Mmm, what time is it?" she asked in a sexy, sleep-laden voice that fueled his desire for her even more.

"Almost six," he said, moving his mouth to nibble on her earlobe. "We're burning daylight."

She chuckled, and the sound reverberated in his chest, making his heart beat faster as it pumped more blood through his veins, directing it farther south. "Slave driver!"

"Not my fault," he said lightly. "But somebody's gotta make sure everything gets done."

They'd been in Montauk, the very tip of Long Island and commonly also known as the Hamptons, staying with his parents for the past few days to make the final arrangements for the wedding. Sabrina seemed more exhausted than usual and he wondered whether the flurry of activities surrounding the wedding was getting to her. He had to admit things were crazy, and what they both needed was a bit of normalcy. And something to ease the stress they were both feeling.

He had just the thing for stress relief. Daniel slid his hand along her torso and down to her belly, pressing her closer into the curve of his body. Sabrina's sigh confirmed that she was fully aware of the hard-on that was now sliding between her thighs and what he intended to do with it.

"Shouldn't we be preserving energy since we have so much to do today?" she murmured, while she rubbed her backside against him and pressed her thighs together to capture his cock between them.

Daniel groaned as her muscles tried to imprison him.

"Trust me, this won't take much of my energy at all," he whispered into her ear and slipped his hand over her sex, cupping it. "It comes naturally." Just like anything to do with Sabrina came naturally.

"Mmm." Her humming was accompanied by her thighs spreading by an inch or two, just enough for him to slip his fingers into her warm center.

"Besides, I think you need this just as much as I do," he added and bathed his fingers in her wetness. Her sex was drenched with her arousal. The scent of it now drifted to him. "Tell me why you're wet already."

"I've been dreaming."

"About?"

"About waking up with you inside me."

Her words made him even harder than he already was. Any more of this and he would explode. "That's a very naughty dream."

His dew-covered finger stroked along her cleft then swept upward to her clit, brushing firmly over the sensitive organ. Sabrina jerked in his arms, a moan dislodging from her lips.

"Yes, I need it," she admitted. "The last few days have been so stressful."

Daniel nuzzled his face in the crook of her neck and inhaled her scent. Sabrina rarely wore perfume. Nevertheless, there was always an enticing scent around her. "Then let me take care of you, baby."

Sabrina lifted her leg a little, allowing him to reposition his cock and tilt it just the right way so it was poised at the entrance to her body.

Keeping his finger rubbing her clit, he thrust his hips up and forward, sliding his cock into her. Sabrina gasped, and the sound echoed in the room. For a brief second he wondered if his parents and the other guests in the house could hear them, but then his attention was pulled back to Sabrina when she slid her hand over his and pressed it harder over her center of pleasure.

A smile formed on his lips. He loved it when Sabrina showed her lusty side. When she urged him on to take her harder, to pleasure her more thoroughly, to drive her wild. Just like she was telling him now that she wanted him to stroke her clit more intensely, with more pressure.

As he caressed the responsive bundle of nerves with circular strokes, he pulled back and sliced into her again. His balls slapped against her flesh, and his cock was lodged deep inside her tight channel. How she could still be so tight even though he'd been making love to her practically every night for the last few months, he didn't know. But he appreciated that fact, because it made every time feel like the first time.

"Fuck," he groaned, drawing out the word.

Daniel steadily plunged in and out of her, stretching her, his tempo increasing. Sabrina met each of his forward thrusts with a backward push of her own, while he continued to caress her clit feverishly, her body now dictating the rhythm of his movements.

He felt sweat build on his neck and torso, making him slide smoothly against Sabrina's back and thighs. He loved taking her like this: the position allowed him total control over her body and satisfied his need to possess every inch of her. It was a feeling that always came over him when she was in his arms. It drove his need for her higher, and made him more adventurous in bed—and out of it—than he'd ever been with anybody else before her.

When he was making love to Sabrina, he knew no boundaries, no limits. Whenever he thought of something that could give her more pleasure, he executed his idea. Her satisfaction was his mission. And whenever she found total satisfaction, he achieved the same fulfillment. Being with Sabrina was perfect in every way.

Just like it was now. Diving into her slick sheath felt like an immersion into liquid silk, into pure heaven. His entire body hummed with pleasure. The nerve endings on this skin vibrated, tingling pleasantly, while his balls burned with the need for release.

In his arms, Sabrina trembled, her body traveling closer and closer toward her climax. He could feel it in the way her breaths became erratic and her sighs and moans increased in frequency and volume. He loved the fact that she expressed herself so freely, that she didn't hold back when she was in his arms.

All of a sudden, Sabrina's interior muscles tightened around his cock.

"Baby, you're killing me," he managed to confess before his brain shut down, robbing him of the ability to speak.

All that mattered now was the sensations flooding his body, the bolts of fire shooting through his core when Sabrina's spasms enveloped him. There was no holding back his orgasm now. With an animalistic groan he plowed into her, allowing the lust for her to overpower him. The last thread of his control snapped, and with another powerful thrust, he shot his seed into her channel, filling her with the hot liquid that seemed to be even more plentiful than usual.

He was unable to stop his movements and continued to slowly drive in and out of her until the waves of her orgasm subsided and his own climax ebbed.

Several shaky breaths tumbled from his mouth, and he tried to use them to form words. But it was useless. Making love to Sabrina always rendered him speechless.

A soft sigh came from her. "Beats sleeping in," she murmured.

Daniel chuckled softly. "Beats a lot of other things, too."

"Can we stay in bed all day?"

He pressed a kiss to her shoulder and pulled out of her. "I wish. But we have guests. Plus there's still tons to organize."

Sabrina let out a long breath. "It's just, I'm so tired at the moment. I could sleep all day."

"When we're on our honeymoon, you can stay in bed all day. I promise you."

She turned her head to look at him. "You still haven't told me where we're going."

"And I won't. But I will tell you that you'll need to pack warm clothes."

Surprise widened her eyes. "We're going somewhere cold?"

He nodded.

"Why somewhere cold? I'd think you'd want to take me somewhere warm and tropical so that I'd have an excuse to walk around half naked."

He winked at her. "Oh, you'll be naked no matter where I take you. If I take you somewhere cold, you won't want to ever leave the hotel or the warmth of the bed. And body heat is the best way to stay warm. Trust me." Then he pushed back the covers and sat up. "Sabrina, baby, I have to shower and get ready. But why don't you stay in bed a little longer? I'll make excuses for you."

She smiled at him. "Have I told you lately that you're the best?"

He leaned down to her. "The best in what?"

She put her arms around his neck, her green eyes beaming at him. "The best in everything." She pressed herself against him. "I can't wait to marry you."

Daniel smiled. "I would have made you my wife months ago, but you deserve a big wedding and to walk down the aisle in a beautiful white gown."

"Every little girl dreams of that."

"And I'll always do everything in my power to fulfill all your dreams."

Reluctantly, he freed himself from her embrace and got out of bed. Naked, he walked toward the bathroom before glancing over his shoulder and finding her running a long look over his backside. She'd never looked more seductive than now—her hair unruly, a rose blush on her cheeks, and the sheets down to her waist, exposing her naked breasts. Tonight, he would bury his head in those generous breasts again and pleasure her with tender strokes and kisses while feeling her nipples harden in his mouth.

That thought alone brought on another hard-on, and he turned away from her to step into the shower.

2

With a spring in his step and in an extremely good mood, Daniel sauntered down the staircase, entering the large foyer of his parents' two-story mansion. He'd loved this place as a kid, because it provided so many opportunities to play hide-and-seek.

He smiled to himself and was about to turn to the left to walk to the kitchen, when something caught his eye on the sideboard near the entrance door. The newspaper lay on it. He grabbed it, wondering why his mother hadn't brought it to the kitchen with her when she'd picked it up from outside where the paperboy normally tossed it onto the driveway. It appeared his mother had just as much going on with the wedding as he and Sabrina did and had probably been distracted by something.

The smell of freshly brewed coffee wafted to him, and he followed it into the kitchen, expecting to see his parents there. But the kitchen was empty. However, his mother had already brewed a large pot of fresh coffee, and the breakfast table was set, though there was no sign or sound from her or his father.

Daniel snatched his favorite mug from the table and poured himself a cup before sitting down, pushing his plate to the side and unfolding the newspaper.

His parents had always gotten the *New York Times* delivered to the house for as long as he could remember, though his mother also read a local newspaper, the *East Hampton Star*, to keep up with the local news. But his father, a businessman like himself, preferred the *Times*.

Daniel flipped through the paper, skipping the "World News" section, then briefly skimmed the business news for anything of interest. He passed over an article discussing a recent business deal his friend and mentor Zach Ivers had struck. Daniel already knew all the details about it, and knew the article couldn't tell him anything he didn't already know.

Knowing he should really go over the lengthy to-do list for the wedding, he folded the various sections which he'd browsed, when his gaze fell onto a photo. He pulled out the section—the weddings and announcements pages—and took a closer look. Why were they running his and Sabrina's picture again when the engagement announcement had been published weeks ago?

When his eyes zeroed in on the headline just above the picture, his heart stuttered to a halt.

Business Tycoon Daniel Sinclair to Marry High-class Call Girl, it read.

His blood turned to ice, while his breath deserted his lungs and his hands gripped the edge of the paper, nearly tearing it.

A little birdie tells me that successful entrepreneur and millionaire Daniel Sinclair, whose equally wealthy family lives in Montauk, NY, has decided to marry outside his class. According to a reliable source, his fiancée, Sabrina Palmer, worked as a high-class escort in San Francisco, where she met Mr. Sinclair, who was a client of the escort service which employed Ms. Palmer. Neither Mr. Sinclair nor Ms. Palmer could be reached for comment.

"Fuck!" Daniel hissed.

Marry outside his class? Sabrina wasn't a call girl! She was as decent a woman as his own mother!

Who the fuck had written these lies? He glanced at the byline: *By Claire Heart – News from the Heart.*

Bullshit! More like news from the gutter! Lies from the gutter!

Fury charged through him. How could this reporter know about how he and Sabrina had met and then twist it into something distasteful? Yes, Sabrina had pretended to be an escort that night, but it hadn't all been like it looked from the outside. It was complicated. And it was certainly not true that Sabrina was a call girl! Despite the circumstances that had brought them together. Were those events going to haunt them forever?

If Sabrina found out about this article, she would be devastated. Wasn't it enough that she'd been embarrassed when he, Daniel, had found out about her initial deception? Now the entire world would find out about what she'd done. And they would judge her. It would destroy her. Not to speak of the wedding which was only days away: knowing

Sabrina, she would cancel it, not wanting to endure the judgmental stares of the community where everybody knew him and his parents, where everybody knew her now, too.

He had to keep this from her and from his parents. Otherwise, the perfect wedding they were planning would turn into utter chaos. And he couldn't allow that. Sabrina deserved a fairytale wedding, and he would do everything to fulfill her wish. Even if that meant keeping this newspaper article from her.

"Good morning, Daniel," his mother's voice suddenly came from the door.

"Uh, morning, Mom!" Daniel jerked his head up and saw his mother enter the kitchen, lifting two shopping bags onto the counter. He used the short time her back was turned to him to hastily fold the remainder of the paper and slide it under the seat cushion of his chair, while he kept talking to drown out any suspicious sounds. "You were already shopping this morning? That's early, even for you. You should have let me know if you needed anything. I would have driven into the village for you later."

His mother looked over her shoulder, while she continued unpacking. She was a short woman, a little over five feet tall, with olive skin and the fiery temperament Italian women were famous for.

"I realized that we were out of coffee creamer. So I went down to the shop quickly. And then I got us some fresh rolls and bread from the bakery while I was down there. Are you the only one up?"

Daniel pasted a smile on his lips, suppressing a sigh of relief that his mother hadn't noticed his clandestine action to hide the newspaper. Now he just had to figure out how to get the newspaper out from its hiding place later, before his mother discovered it after breakfast.

"Sabrina is taking a shower. She'll be down soon. But I haven't heard anybody else up yet. Is Dad still sleeping?"

His mother chuckled. "Are you kidding? He's already gone for a swim. He's in the shower right now." She placed an assortment of rolls and slices of fresh bread into a basket, grabbed the coffee creamer and carried both to the table. "Here! Try these rolls."

"Thanks, Mom! They look delicious." If only he were hungry, but that damned newspaper article had ruined his appetite. All he could do was sip more of his black coffee. And even that tasted bitter this morning, though he was sure it wasn't his mother's fault. She always made excellent coffee and insisted on buying only an Italian brand, Illy.

"Did you see the newspaper?" she suddenly asked, craning her neck to look around the kitchen.

"No, why?" Daniel hoped he didn't sound phony. He hated lying to his mother, but he couldn't help it. It was paramount that nobody read the paper this morning, or all hell would break loose.

"It wasn't on the table in the foyer anymore when I got home."

"Hmm. I didn't see anything when I came down. Maybe you didn't bring it in."

She shook her head. "No, I'm sure I brought it in when I went out this morning."

He shrugged and reached for a roll to give his hands something to do and look relaxed. "If you were on your way out, why would you have come back in to put the newspaper on the table?"

"Daniel, I remember what I did! Don't make it sound like I'm having a senior moment!"

He bent to her and pressed a kiss on her cheek. "Sorry, Mom. I'm sure it'll turn up. Maybe the paperboy missed our house. You know how kids are these days. No sense of responsibility anymore."

He sent a silent apology to the falsely-accused paperboy who'd done nothing wrong other than deliver an edition of the *New York Times* that nobody in Daniel's family could be allowed to read.

Then he cut the roll in half and spread butter on it. "Thanks for preparing breakfast for all of us. I know you're busy. I really appreciate everything you're doing for us."

Instantly, his mother's face lit up. "It's so exciting to plan a wedding!"

"I think your mother means exhausting, not exciting," Tim's voice came from the door, as he entered the kitchen, Holly on his heels.

"You haven't even done anything yet, Tim!" Holly rolled her eyes and tossed a strand of her long blonde hair over her shoulder.

"I know, but I can totally imagine it, and the thought alone exhausts me." Tim grinned unashamedly. His old college friend from Princeton was partially responsible for Daniel meeting Sabrina. The other half of the responsibility fell on Holly, Sabrina's old roommate from San

Francisco. Together the two had hatched a plot to set him and Sabrina up on a blind date. It had worked in the end, albeit with a few hitches.

Tim bent down to Daniel's mother and kissed her on the cheek. "Good morning, Raffaela. Sorry, we didn't get to say hello last night when we got in."

She hugged him back, then stood to embrace Holly. "It's such a hassle these days with delayed flights. At least you flew into JFK, so you weren't as far as if you'd flown into Newark."

"Morning, Raffaela," Holly greeted her, then took a seat at the breakfast table next to Tim. "Well, at least we made it." She reached for the coffee pot and poured herself a cup. "And the guestroom is just lovely. I slept like a baby."

A ravishing smile spread over his mother's lips at Holly's compliment. Holly always knew how to charm Daniel's mother. Holly was a true beauty with sparkling blue eyes and could have had any man she wanted. Why she wasted her life as a professional escort—a fact Daniel's parents weren't aware of—Daniel couldn't quite figure out. Wasn't she sick of sleeping with strangers?

"Oh, thank you, dear. And, Tim, did you sleep all right?"

"I slept great! And now I could eat a whole cow!"

His mother chuckled. "How about part of a pig? I have sausages and bacon being kept warm in the oven."

"Perfect!"

When his mother was about to leap from her chair, Tim put a hand on her forearm. "Sit, sit. I'll get it. It's not like I don't know my way around here."

As Tim walked to the oven and opened it to take out the pan, Daniel's father and Sabrina entered the kitchen. His father didn't look all that different from Daniel—though his hair was the color of salt and pepper now. But his body was still as athletic as it had been in his thirties.

Within moments, everybody was sitting at the breakfast table, eating and chatting. Sabrina had taken a seat next to him, and Daniel looked at her from the side. Yes, he would make sure she would get her fairytale wedding. No matter what.

He reached up with his hand, brushing a strand of her long dark hair behind her shoulder. Sabrina turned to meet his gaze.

"What?" she murmured.

"Nothing, baby. I just can't stop looking at you," he responded just as quietly.

"You're not on your honeymoon yet," Tim said in a teasing voice.

Holly jabbed her elbow into Tim's side. "I think it's sweet. If only every girl were as lucky as Sabrina."

Sabrina smiled at her friend. "Thank you, Holly."

"So, what's on the agenda today?" Tim asked as he scooped more food onto his plate.

Before anybody could answer, Daniel's father asked, "Where's the paper, honey? Didn't you bring it in?"

Daniel tried not to cringe. He'd hoped his father wouldn't notice the absence of the newspaper since the conversation over breakfast was even more lively than usual, considering they had two out-of-town houseguests.

"I thought I did, but apparently my days are running together. I can't seem to find it anywhere."

"Did you check outside?" his father pressed.

"Of course I checked outside. Twice, when I left for the bakery and when I got back."

"I don't think the paper was delivered today," Daniel threw in.

"What do you mean it wasn't delivered? Forty-some-odd years we've lived here and that paper has always been delivered."

"The paperboy probably screwed up. Maybe it's a new kid," Daniel offered.

"Why don't you just read the paper on your iPad?" Tim asked, nodding toward the device on the counter.

Daniel wanted to groan loudly. Sometimes Tim could be a little too helpful.

His father snapped his fingers and smiled doubtfully. "Yeah. I always forget I can do that. But you know, I kind of like the feel of the paper."

"You mean getting all that black ink on your fingers? I only read the paper online now. All you need to do is get a subscription to the *New York Times*. It's cheaper than the paper version anyway," Tim claimed.

Not wanting this conversation to go any further and give Tim another chance to convince Daniel's father to take out an online subscription, Daniel pasted a smile on his face and said, "Well, I don't think anybody here has time to read the paper today anyway. We've got a full agenda. Don't we, baby?" He smiled at Sabrina.

"Don't remind me!" Sabrina sighed. "We have to meet with the pianist to give final approval of the music. And then we have to head over to the florist. She has a sample bouquet ready for us to look at."

"How exciting!" Holly's face lit up. "The flowers you chose are absolutely gorgeous."

"Believe it or not . . . " Sabrina looked at Daniel and smiled. " . . . they were Daniel's choice."

"It's nice to know Daniel learned something from me after all these years," Raffaela said wistfully.

"I also have to go for a dress fitting, but I think I'll push that to tomorrow or the day after," Sabrina added. "Are you coming with me, Holly?"

Holly nodded enthusiastically. "Why do you think I flew in over a week early?"

One of the decisions Daniel and Sabrina had made early on was to keep the ceremony small and intimate. So, other than the bride and groom, the wedding party comprised only two other people: Tim, his best man, and Holly, the maid of honor.

Of course, Daniel's mother had gone overboard with the guest list. Daniel and Sabrina had agreed to allow her this one indulgence. Over two hundred guests had been invited, the list comprising distant relatives, friends of the family, friends of Daniel, as well as Sabrina's divorced parents and a few of her friends and relatives from the West Coast.

"I can't believe the wedding is only ten days away," Holly said, ripping Daniel from his thoughts. "It seems like yesterday that you two met."

Daniel groaned mentally. If he didn't do damage control swiftly, everybody would soon know how he and Sabrina had met. Then the lie they had told his parents would be revealed, and he wasn't sure how they would take the news. Nor did he think that Sabrina would survive the scrutiny she would suddenly be subjected to. It would devastate her.

"I know." Sabrina sighed as she reached over and took Daniel's hand. "I'm excited, but a bit overwhelmed by everything that still needs to be done."

Daniel squeezed her hand then brought it to his lips, kissing her knuckles. "Don't worry, baby. Reinforcements are here." He motioned to Tim and Holly.

Both of them would be a great help with the preparations and take the heat off Sabrina.

Sabrina laughed. "Yes, I'd be lost without my posse," she teased.

"Well, while the girls are dealing with music and flowers, I thought maybe you and I could discuss the bachelor party," Tim said, pinning Daniel with a look that he couldn't avoid.

That was another thing—Daniel didn't want a bachelor party, at least not a traditional one. For many years he'd been one of New York's most eligible bachelors, but it was a title he was happy to rid himself of. The idea of celebrating his last night as a single man seemed ironic and unnecessary. He was thrilled to be getting married, to never have to fend off another gold-digging socialite.

But Tim had insisted that there would be a party. Daniel had finally agreed to indulge him, but had made it clear: no strippers and no trips to Las Vegas.

"Actually, can we discuss the party tomorrow?" Daniel said with an apologetic look. "I'm going to have to excuse myself from the wedding planning today."

"What? Why?" Sabrina's head snapped in his direction.

He gave her a reassuring smile. "I received an urgent message from work this morning. I have to drive to New York today and deal with it," he lied.

From the look on Sabrina's face he could tell that she was not pleased—and rightfully so. He should stay here and pull his weight, taking some of the pressure off her shoulders. "I'm sorry, Sabrina, but I'd much rather deal with this right now than a day or two before the wedding. I'll make sure they know that after today, I'll be unreachable."

"Why can't you just tell them that now?" Sabrina asked.

Daniel cupped her cheek and caressed her face with his thumb. "Please understand, baby. This is something I have to take care of. I promise you, I'll be back tonight, and then the four of us can go out and do something."

Sabrina sighed. "Okay. I guess it won't matter." She motioned to Holly and Tim. "At least Holly and Tim can help your mother and me out."

"Perfect."

Daniel hated having to leave, but he knew he had to. Because the more he thought about it, the more he knew what he had to do. He wouldn't stand idly by and let this reporter get away with her lies. He would find out who exactly Claire Heart's *reliable source* was, and get a retraction and an apology published. Only then would he feel at ease and know his and Sabrina's happiness would be assured.

And by the time he and Sabrina got back from their honeymoon, things would have blown over, and everybody would have forgotten about the article. Another scandal would capture people's attention. And Sabrina would never know.

3

Daniel jumped out of his sports car and stretched his legs. He'd practically raced from Montauk to Manhattan and was lucky not to have gotten any speeding tickets on the way.

The office building of the *New York Times* was located on Eighth Avenue in the center of Hell's Kitchen. Daniel looked up at the glass wall that sported large black letters, spelling out the newspaper's name in its trademark font. The sun reflected on the glass.

He straightened his tie and entered the building, heading straight for the security desk. The African American man in the impeccable dark suit looked at him.

"How may I help you, sir?" he said, his voice polite yet firm.

"I'd like to see Miss Claire Heart."

He looked down at his computer screen, already typing something. "And your name, sir?"

"Daniel Sinclair."

The man perused the screen for a few moments then looked up again. "I'm afraid I don't have your appointment registered here. When—"

"I don't have an appointment," Daniel interrupted, leaning over the counter.

"I'm afraid I can only let you in if you have an appointment."

"Miss Heart will want to speak to me. I assure you."

"Be that as it may, the rules are the rules. Please come back when you have an appointment."

Daniel pointed to the phone on his desk. "Call her. Now. She's been looking for me to comment on her story, and she will be upset if you send me away. This is her only chance to get my comment," he bluffed, underlining his words with a stoic expression that gave nothing away of the storm that still raged inside him. In fact, the storm had just hit hurricane strength.

For a moment, the security guard hesitated, clearly contemplating Daniel's claim. Then he picked up the phone and dialed a number.

"Miss Heart, this is Barry from security downstairs. I've got a Mr. Sinclair here who wants to comment on one of your stories. He doesn't have an appointment, but he claims—" Barry pulled back his shoulders, sitting up even straighter. "Yes, Ma'am." He nodded. "Right away." Then he put the phone down and looked down at his desk, writing something.

Impatiently, Daniel tapped his foot on the floor, when finally Barry looked up at him and handed him a visitor pass to pin to his jacket.

"Miss Heart is on the ninth floor. Please take elevator four." He pointed to an elevator bank behind Daniel.

"Thank you." Daniel pinned the visitor pass to the lapel of his jacket and walked to the elevator. It opened when he reached it, and he stepped inside.

He didn't have to press the button for the ninth floor. It was already lit, and he knew that the security guard had programmed it so that Daniel could alight only on the ninth floor and not roam around anywhere else in the building. Most large office buildings had this security feature.

During the ride up, he tried to calm his mind. It would serve nobody if he yelled at the gossip columnist. He needed to get her onto his side, not alienate her.

The elevator doors opened on the ninth floor, and he stepped into the hallway.

"Mr. Sinclair," a petite brunette greeted him. She was dressed in casual pants and a colorful blouse. Her hand was stretched toward him in greeting. "I'm Claire Heart."

"Good afternoon, Miss Heart." He shook her hand briefly. "Thank you for seeing me on such short notice. I'm here about your article that ran in today's paper."

Claire nodded. "Oh, I know why you're here. Let's go to my office where we can talk in private."

He followed her as she led him down a long corridor, surprised that she was so accommodating. Moments later, she entered a tiny office with stacks of papers, magazines and files lining the walls and littering the floor.

"Excuse the mess. I've just moved offices." She walked around the surprisingly empty desk with only a date book and a telephone on it and sat down on the chair behind it, pointing to the only other chair in the room. "Please, Mr. Sinclair."

He took a seat and waited for a few seconds, trying to read her facial expression. But she gave nothing away. If she was aware that the story she'd printed was a lie, she didn't let on.

"I want you to issue a retraction of your story."

Claire leaned forward slightly. "And why would I do that?"

"Because the story is a lie. My fiancée is not a call girl. And had you bothered to ask for comment from me before you published the story, I could have cleared all this up beforehand and saved us all a lot of trouble."

"I did ask for comment! You declined!" Claire insisted.

"I never even received a request for comment from you, Miss Heart! So, let's stick to the truth here."

She narrowed her eyes in displeasure. "I contacted your office, Mr. Sinclair, and was informed that you were unavailable for comment. Guess what: I took that to mean you were *unavailable for comment,*" she said snidely.

Daniel wasn't sure the reporter was telling the truth. His assistant Frances was extremely reliable and would have passed a message like this along, even though he had instructed his office not to disturb him during the week before his wedding. "Never mind that now. The issue remains that you published a story that simply has no basis in fact."

"I have a very credible source who convinced both me and my editor."

Daniel leaned forward. "Who?"

"You know as well as I do that I have to protect the identity of my sources."

"Your source is lying. My fiancée never was and never will be a call girl. She is a respectable attorney."

Claire crossed her arms over her chest. "I'm afraid, Mr. Sinclair, I've been shown concrete proof that Miss Parker worked as a call girl in San Francisco. And I also have concrete proof that you hired her as such."

Inside, Daniel was seething. "I will find out who your source is. My lawyers—"

The ringing of Claire's phone interrupted him.

"One moment," she said, looked at the number on the display, and reached for it. "I'll have to take this."

She lifted the receiver to her ear. "Yes, Rick, what is it now?" Impatience colored her voice.

Daniel heard a loud male voice through the line, but couldn't make out the words.

Claire shoved a hand through her hair. "I told them already! I met my source on . . . hold on." She leafed through the day planner on her desk, searching for an entry. Finally, she tapped onto a spot on the paper. "There! I met with my source on the twenty-third."

Again, the man on the other line said something, while Daniel stared at the day planner. She noted her meetings with her sources on this calendar? Interesting.

Claire sighed. "Fine! I'll be up in a few minutes." Then she put down the receiver and looked back at him. "As I said, the story is solid. I won't retract it, because it's the truth. And just because you don't like it, won't make it otherwise."

"Fine, Miss Heart. If that's how you want to play this." Daniel stood. "The *New York Times* wouldn't be the first newspaper to get destroyed by a libel suit."

"It's not libel if it's true. I stand by my article and my source."

"Very well. I'll see myself out." He turned to the door and left her office, closing the door behind him.

His eyes scanned the doors along the corridor as he hurried in the direction of the elevator. Finally he saw what he was looking for: the men's room. He dove into it and was relieved to find it empty. No sounds came from the three stalls.

Daniel remained at the door, keeping it ajar so he could spy into the corridor. He didn't have to wait long. Moments later Claire Heart walked past the door in hasty steps, heading for the elevator. When he heard the elevator ping, he counted to five, then stepped back into the hallway, his eyes immediately scanning the area near the elevators. Claire was gone.

Relieved, he walked back in the direction of her office, adrenalin pumping through his veins. He'd never in his life done anything illegal, but he had no choice today. He needed to find out who the reporter's source was. He felt like a burglar when he slid back into Claire's office and walked around her desk. With one eye he scanned the pages of her day planner, with the other he watched the door.

The annotations in Miss Heart's calendar were cryptic. She used lots of abbreviations, and the names of her sources, or whomever she met with, were only initials. Clearly, she wanted to make sure that if this date book fell into the wrong hands, she wouldn't reveal the names of her confidential sources.

Daniel worked backwards, knowing that no reporter sat on a juicy story for very long. Claire would have to have met her source sometime within the last two weeks. It would have given her enough time to verify whatever evidence had been presented to her. Evidence? He huffed. There was no evidence. Whatever Claire had received was fabricated. Daniel would find the source and prove that the claims were a lie.

With determination, he read each and every entry for the last two weeks, when he suddenly stumbled over initials that triggered a memory in him. A suitcase with the initials *AH* engraved on the lock appeared before his mind's eye. He'd seen that suitcase so many times, had in fact carried it often.

The entry was on the tenth of the month at two thirty in the afternoon and read: *AH re: DS cg.*

He could only interpret this to mean: *Audrey Hawkins regarding Daniel Sinclair, call girl.*

Who else could it be? It had to be Audrey! She was the only one who still held such a deep grudge against him that she would try to destroy his happiness with Sabrina. He and Audrey had once been an item. With Audrey being the quintessential socialite, he'd once thought that they were the perfect couple. After all, they both belonged to the same upper class circles of New York. But for all her beauty and obvious charms, he'd never truly been in love with Audrey and had often traded dinner and sex with her for late-night business meetings.

Their breakup had been inevitable, though the way it had happened had surprised even Daniel: he'd found Audrey fucking his attorney.

Daniel had broken it off right there and then and fired his attorney in the same instant. But Audrey hadn't given up so easily.

When she'd followed him on a business trip to San Francisco in the hope of winning him back, she'd discovered him with Sabrina. Things had gotten ugly and nearly destroyed his already-shaky beginnings with Sabrina. And it appeared now that Audrey was still not done. She was still trying to destroy his relationship with Sabrina.

But he wouldn't let her succeed.

Daniel charged out of the office, not caring if anybody saw him now. He'd gotten the information he needed. Nobody could stop him now.

Outside, he rushed to where he'd parked his car and sped away.

He could of course call Audrey on the phone, but what would be the point? She wouldn't pick up the phone when she recognized the number. Besides, he wanted to confront her in person, because it was much easier to intimidate her face-to-face.

During the entire drive to her midtown co-op, rage tore through him. He'd thought that after the last confrontation with Audrey, which had nearly destroyed his relationship with Sabrina, she would have finally given up. However, it appeared that Audrey wasn't done with her games.

The doorman in Audrey's building called up to her apartment and then allowed him to ride upstairs. If Audrey was trying to pull the same seduction scene she'd tried on him once before, then she would get a nasty surprise. He wasn't susceptible to her charms anymore. He hadn't been for a long time.

At the door to her apartment, Daniel was greeted by Audrey's housekeeper, Betty. Her face lit up when she saw him. He liked the older woman and felt sorry for her that she had to work for somebody like Audrey, who couldn't possibly be a pleasant employer.

"Oh, Mr. Sinclair, how nice to see you again!"

He forced himself to be civil to her. After all, it wasn't her fault that her employer was devious and heartless. "Hi, Betty. It's nice to see you, too. I'm here to see Audrey. It's important."

"I'm sorry, but she's not here."

"Not here?" He stepped past Betty, entering the foyer that opened up to a large sunken living room. He cast a look around, but the room was empty and looking just as gaudy as ever. He'd never shared Audrey's taste for over-the-top extravagance.

Behind him, Betty closed the door. "Did she know you were coming? She must have forgotten. I'm afraid she left rather abruptly two days ago."

He turned to Betty. "Where to?"

The housekeeper shrugged. "She said she was going on a trip, that she needed some time to sort things out. But she didn't mention where to. And I know better than to ask. You know Miss Audrey."

Of course he did. He knew exactly what she was like.

Daniel pulled his cell phone from his pocket and found her number. The phone rang several times before it went to voicemail. He didn't bother leaving a message and simply disconnected the call with a curse.

He caught Betty's concerned look when he looked up.

"Is she in some sort of trouble?"

"She will be once I find her," Daniel ground out.

4

"Are you sure you're okay with this?" Holly asked.

"Yes, I'll be fine." Sabrina laughed. "Now go." She shooed Holly away.

"Okay. Call us as soon as you're finished with the pianist and we'll meet up." Holly gave Sabrina a hug, and then turned to Raffaela. "Ready?"

Raffaela nodded and looked at Sabrina. "We can stay and help you if you want us to."

Sabrina rolled her eyes in an exaggerated way. "It doesn't take three of us to go over the music arrangements. The pianist and I can handle it just fine. You two go shopping or whatever it is you plan to do."

"You know me too well." Holly winked and looped her arm through Raffaela's.

She felt a bit guilty about leaving Sabrina to deal with the music on her own, but Raffaela had asked for Holly's help and since it involved shopping, she simply couldn't resist.

Once outside and out of earshot of Sabrina, Holly addressed Raffaela, "So, do you have any idea what you'd like to get for Sabrina?"

"No." Raffaela sighed. "I want to get her a special wedding gift, something personal and heartfelt, but I really have no idea what to get her." She laughed. "That's why I brought you along, so you could help me pick something out. You know her much better than I do."

Holly smiled. "I'm sure we can find something."

She opened the car door and slid into the passenger seat of Raffaela's car. Raffaela pulled out of the driveway and headed toward East Hampton. Raffaela had told her earlier that Montauk didn't have much to offer in terms of shopping, and that they would have more of a selection in East Hampton.

"I'm so grateful to you and Tim for introducing them," Raffaela started. "I've never seen my son so happy."

Holly smiled wistfully. If only Raffaela knew under what circumstances her son had met Sabrina, she would probably not thank her as enthusiastically. Most likely she'd be appalled. Horrified. Maybe even disgusted. Just as well that she didn't know what she, Holly, did for a living.

"We thought they would be good together. And they are."

Raffaela chuckled. "Yes, they are so cute together. It reminds me of when James and I met. We were just as much in love as those two. So how about you, Holly? Do you have anybody special?"

Holly looked out of the window as they drove along Montauk Highway. Windswept dunes interspersed with beautiful houses farther back from the highway caught her eye. Would she one day live in a house like that? She doubted it. After all, she didn't lead the kind of respectable life these people did. Her life was so different. For the first time she wondered whether it was time to make a change, to stop what she was doing and turn her back on it.

"I?" Holly laughed to cover up her feelings of longing for a relationship. "There are too many fabulous guys out there. Who can make a choice and pick one? It's like an endless buffet. There are so many goodies that in the end you don't know what to eat."

Raffaela laughed out loud. "You're so funny, Holly! But you're right. You're still young. You should play the field and not settle for the first guy who comes along." She leaned closer. "With your looks you can get anybody you want."

Holly smiled. "That's very nice of you to say."

Certainly, her looks had made her one of the most requested girls at Misty's escort service. She could command a high price for her services. But was the price that *Holly* had to pay getting too high? Was she wasting her best years in an occupation that would eventually lead into a dead end? She knew that none of the clients she met as an escort would ever look at her as marriage material. Because she wasn't. She wasn't respectable. What she did wasn't only illegal in most states, it was considered indecent. And no man in his right mind would ever consider a relationship with somebody like her.

While not all assignments at the escort agency involved sex, many of them did. What man would pay the price her boss charged for just an evening of conversation? And even though Holly had the right to refuse a guy and back out of an assignment if she found the man in question distasteful, she couldn't play this get-out-of-jail-free card every time— eventually Misty would fire her, because only bookings involving sex brought in the big bucks.

Sometimes Holly enjoyed her sexual encounters with the men who hired her, but it happened less and less that she felt good about what she did. If she didn't get out of it while she still could, she knew what would eventually happen. She would have wasted her best years. And she would end up alone.

"So what do you say?"

Holly snapped her head back to Raffaela, realizing that she had tuned out while wallowing in her thoughts. "Hmm?"

"The jewelry store. I figured we'd go there first."

"Jewelry is always a great idea," Holly agreed and looked around.

They had reached downtown East Hampton. Raffaela pulled into a parking spot along the street and turned off the engine. "We're here."

"This is really quaint!" Holly exclaimed as she sauntered from the car.

Downtown East Hampton wasn't large. In fact, it consisted of merely a main street lined by several shops and a few side streets. Surprisingly classy boutiques stood next to local eateries and Mom-and-Pop stores. Clearly, the rich New Yorkers who spent their summers in the Hamptons didn't want to get withdrawal symptoms from shopping while they vacationed here.

Holly took it all in. It looked so different from San Francisco and the West Coast. Almost as if cut out from a picture book. To her surprise, she liked it. It gave her a feeling of home, of warmth and belonging. She shook off the thought. Obviously, dealing with Sabrina's wedding was making her soft when she was the toughest cookie out there. Sentimentality wasn't her game. She was direct and practical. Not girly and emotional, despite what her blonde model looks might suggest.

"This way," Raffaela instructed and walked along the sidewalk.

Holly joined her, walking alongside her until they reached a small jewelry store. Raffaela entered amidst a soothing chime sounding overhead. As Holly entered the small store behind her, she glanced around. The room they stood in was tiny, and the display cases were filled with what looked like antique jewelry. Heirlooms from estate sales, she assumed. It appeared that the store specialized in old pieces.

Holly cast Raffaela a curious glance. She'd expected Sabrina's future mother-in-law to go to a fancy jewelry store and buy her something pretty but ordinary. But by the looks of it, Raffaela had put more thought into it than Holly had expected.

While the man behind the counter was talking to a customer, he quickly nodded to them, apparently recognizing Raffaela.

"This is an unusual place," Holly whispered to Raffaela, not wanting to speak too loudly, because somehow she felt as if she were intruding in somebody's living room, so welcoming and inviting was the store.

Raffaela smiled. "It's been here forever."

Then she dug into the bottom of her purse and pulled out a tiny, black velvet bag. She opened it and took out a sparkling green emerald, holding it up to show it to Holly. Holly had always thought of emeralds being rather murky, but this one sparkled brighter than she'd ever seen an emerald sparkle.

"It belonged to Daniel's grandmother. It was the stone in her wedding band. She loved Daniel. In her will she passed it on to me for safekeeping until I could pass it on to Daniel's wife. How do you think we should have it set?"

Holly stared at the precious gem. "It's so beautiful. Just like Sabrina's eyes," she whispered with awe. "I think a necklace would do it most justice."

"You don't think it's too impersonal?"

"No, not at all. Once you tell Sabrina the story behind it, it will bring her to tears. I guarantee it."

"A necklace it is."

They had to wait for another few minutes until the store's owner was available to serve them.

"Good morning, Mr. Anderson."

The man nodded and smiled broadly at the two of them. "Mrs. Sinclair. So nice to see you again." He inclined his head toward Holly. "Ma'am. How may I help you two pretty ladies?"

Raffaela chuckled. "You charmer!" She placed the gemstone onto the velvet cushion on the counter in front of Mr. Anderson. "I'd like to have this stone set into a necklace for my future daughter-in-law. Do you think that's possible?"

"Anything is possible." He lifted the stone and inspected it closely. "Beautiful. An exceptional clarity. I would suggest white gold with it. Or platinum." He looked up. "I could make you a beautiful design with this."

"I'm afraid we don't have time to have something designed. The wedding is in ten days."

"Oh." He rubbed the back of his neck with his free hand. "In that case, let's have a look through the collection and see what necklace would benefit from a stone like this." He waved them both to another display case along the wall.

In it, antique necklaces rubbed shoulders with sets of earrings and brooches. Holly stared at the jewelry. Every single piece was beautifully crafted and unique.

"This one!" Raffaela pointed to a necklace with delicate gold swirls, in the center of which small sparkling diamonds sat. The center of the piece housed a ruby.

"Good choice, Mrs. Sinclair." Mr. Anderson lifted the lid and took out the necklace. "I think all I'll need to do is replace the center with a slightly larger setting to accommodate the emerald. I can have it ready in four days, five maximum."

Raffaela turned to Holly. "What do you think?"

Holly smiled back at her. "She'll love it."

When they stepped out of the shop a short while later, Holly turned to Raffaela. "I can't possibly top your present for Sabrina, but I figured I'd get her something for the honeymoon. I was thinking lingerie."

Raffaela chuckled. "You mean a present for Daniel?"

Holly laughed. "Well, if you put it that way, a present for both of them."

"I know just the place. There's an adorable little boutique at the end of the block. I'm sure you'll find what you're looking for in there."

They walked to the lingerie store and entered. Holly looked around, surprised by how large it was. Apparently the residents of this sleepy town were into their nightly entertainment in order to keep a place like this in business. "Wow. This place is great."

"I knew you'd like it."

Holly looked around with an open mouth. This was like her personal heaven. She loved lingerie, always had, even before she'd become an escort and having beautiful lingerie had become a necessity. Maybe she would not only buy Sabrina something nice, but also get something for herself. After all, she couldn't let an opportunity like this pass her by.

Stopping at a display of long, silk negligees, Holly browsed through them then reached for one and pulled it out. A soft pink negligee reaching to mid-thigh and held up by spaghetti straps had Sabrina's name all over it. It was classy, elegant, yet sexy. It looked like it had been tailored specifically for Sabrina's body.

"Raffaela, look. This is it." She turned to show it to Raffaela.

"Oh, Holly, that's perfect." Raffaela clapped her hands, a huge smile taking over her face.

"Sold! Now, I just need to find something for myself. It would be a shame not to." But before she could turn to the next display, a woman turned to them.

"Raffaela? Wow! What a surprise to see you here!"

"Linda," Raffaela greeted her with a rather tight smile, which surprised Holly, since she'd never seen her being unfriendly to anybody. Yet Holly could instantly feel that Raffaela didn't care for the woman she'd called Linda. "How nice to see you."

When Linda cast a curious glance over Holly, Raffaela continued, "Linda this is Holly, Sabrina's best friend and maid of honor. Holly, this is Linda Boyd, a family friend."

"Nice to meet you, Linda." Holly extended her hand and was greeted with a stiff smile and a weak shake, while the woman continued to look her up and down as if inspecting a cheap garment.

"Likewise," Linda said, immediately turning her attention back to Raffaela. "I'm surprised to see you out shopping. I thought for sure you'd be too busy with everything else."

"We're shopping for the wedding, actually," Raffaela responded calmly.

Linda's plastic smile never faded as she leaned closer as if wanting to impart a secret without being overheard. "Uh, yes. Speaking of the wedding, isn't this whole thing just awful? People can be so nasty at times."

"What do you mean?" Raffaela looked at Linda in confusion. "My son is getting married. And there's nothing awful about that."

Linda shook her head. "Of course not, but that article in the paper today, the one about Sabrina . . . I was shocked when I read it. Of course, I don't believe a word of it."

"I'm afraid we didn't get the paper this morning, so I'm not sure what article you're talking about."

Holly could hear the edge in Raffaela's voice.

"Oh." Linda put her hand over her mouth in an attempt to look surprised. "You mean . . . you don't know about the article in the *New York Times*? Oh, dear. I didn't mean to bring it up. I'm sorry."

"Linda, what is this about?"

"Gosh, Raffaela, I'm so sorry. I didn't mean to be the one giving you bad news. I just assumed you knew, because it's all everyone is talking about all morning. I'm sure it's all a big mistake. I mean it can't be true." She put her hand on Raffaela's forearm. "Listen, just forget about it. I'm so sorry."

Then she turned abruptly and left the store, leaving Raffaela standing with a frown on her face. Holly turned to Raffaela. When their gazes met, Raffaela said, "I need to buy a newspaper."

Holly nodded numbly. Something was wrong. She tossed the negligee back on the display case and took Raffaela's arm. "Let's get to the bottom of this."

As they walked outside and headed for the next newspaper stand, Holly glanced at Raffaela.

"I know Linda is a family friend, but I don't like that woman very much."

"Not many people do. She's a gossip. I've tried to keep her at a distance since Daniel's breakup with Audrey, but in a place like the Hamptons, that's not always so easy."

"What does Linda have to do with Daniel's breakup with Audrey?"

"Linda and Audrey are close."

Holly's stomach lurched. A friend of Audrey's was delivering bad news about Sabrina? What were the odds of that being a coincidence?

At the newsstand, Raffaela dropped several coins into the box and snatched a copy of the *New York Times* from it. Holly followed her as she headed for the car, unlocking it and getting in, before unfolding the paper.

She handed Holly half the sections. "You check these parts, I'll check the others."

Hastily Holly flipped through section after section, scanning the headlines and looking at every picture, when she suddenly heard Raffaela gasp.

Holly whirled her head to her and instantly noticed how her face had paled, her eyes widened, and her jaw dropped.

"Raffaela? What is it?" Holly peered at the spot Raffaela was staring at. Her eyes focused, and her breath caught in her chest. "Oh my god!"

This couldn't be happening!

"Promise me not to tell Sabrina about any of this. I have to talk to Daniel first," Raffaela said.

Holly nodded, full of guilt. If she hadn't come up with this harebrained idea of letting Sabrina pretend to be an escort, this would never have happened.

5

Over the hands-free system in his car, he heard the phone ring twice, until his attorney Elliott Langdon answered. "Daniel?"

"Elliott, listen, something happened. I need you to do something for me and—"

"I was expecting your call. Let me guess: you want to sue the *New York Times*?" Elliott interrupted.

"Then you know what's going on." At least it meant that he didn't have to launch into lengthy explanations about the article.

"I nearly choked on my toast this morning. I'm assuming it's all fabrication?"

"Yes. I've already spoken to the reporter, Claire Heart."

"What's she got?"

"She wouldn't reveal it, but I figured out who her source is."

"Who?"

"Audrey Hawkins."

He heard Elliott whistle through his teeth. "Not giving up, is she? Well, in that case, let's get to Audrey and force her to give us what she has."

Daniel sighed. "Tried that already. She's disappeared. She knew I'd find out and come after her."

"In that case, I'll start with the legal counsel of the *New York Times*. I know one of the attorneys on their team. Let me talk to him and see what I can find out."

"Good, but don't make any waves yet. I don't want to launch a lawsuit before the wedding. It would cause too much attention." And it would mean that Sabrina would find out for certain.

"No worries, I know how to handle this."

"Thanks, Elliott. In the meantime, I'll try to find Audrey. Knowing her, she didn't go far. She would want to be around to enjoy the chaos she created."

"Sounds like her. I'll call you when I know more."

"Thanks."

Daniel disconnected the call and concentrated on traffic.

He'd already called several of her friends and acquaintances, asking them about Audrey's whereabouts, but nobody had heard of her. All claimed that they didn't know where she was.

On the drive to the Hamptons, he continued to make phone call after phone call, but none of their mutual acquaintances had seen her.

By the time Daniel pulled into the driveway of his parents' house, he was exhausted. Physically, mentally, and emotionally.

Daniel got out of his car, shut the door and locked the car. It was early evening, and the sun was just starting to set. A walk along the beach with Sabrina, watching the sun go down, would be just what he needed to calm his nerves.

Before Daniel could put his key into the front door, it was opened from the inside. Both his parents stood in the entrance, their faces masks of worry. His stomach clenched. Something had happened.

"Mom, Dad. What's going on? Is Sabrina all right?" he asked, darting looks past them into the house. It was unusually quiet.

His mother nodded. "Tim and Holly took Sabrina for a walk on the beach."

"So we might talk without Sabrina overhearing us," his father added cryptically.

Panic and dread collided inside him. "What's going on?"

His parents motioned him inside, ushering him into his father's study, which was located off the foyer. Only when his father had closed the door behind him, did he speak again.

"This is serious, Daniel."

Daniel raked his hand through his hair. As if he didn't have enough problems already.

"I ran into Linda Boyd today," his mother started. "She told me about the article in the *New York Times*."

Shit!

If Linda knew, then everyone knew. He should have known he wouldn't be able to keep the article a secret for long.

He let out a sigh.

"So you know about the article," his mother continued.

"Is it true? Is Sabrina a call girl?" his father asked.

"No, of course not." Daniel glared at his father. "Sabrina is a respectable woman! She's not a call girl!"

"Then why would the paper run a story like that?"

"I don't know." Daniel sighed. "That's why I went to the city today. To try and find out. I talked to that gossip columnist, Claire Heart."

"And? Is she going to retract the story?" his mother pressed. Her tone and her eyes were hopeful.

He hated to disappoint her. "No. She claims she has solid evidence. And she wouldn't give up her source."

"But what proof can there be when Sabrina isn't a call girl? How can they print something like that? No editor in his right mind would let a reporter get away with that. They must have some sort of evidence," his father insisted.

"They have nothing, because there's nothing they can possibly know."

His father narrowed his eyes. "What are you not telling us?"

Daniel took a few deep breaths. Maybe it was time to come clean. His father was a reasonable man with a bright head on his shoulders. He wouldn't condemn him and Sabrina for what they'd done.

"The source is Audrey," he bit out. "I found an entry in the reporter's day planner, confirming that she met with Audrey just a few days ago."

"You found it in her day planner?" his father asked with a raised eyebrow. "Did you do something illegal?"

Daniel shrugged. "Dad, I don't think trespassing is my biggest problem right now. Besides, nobody saw me."

His mother slapped a hand over her mouth, choking back a gasp, while his father, a pragmatist at heart, shrugged.

"Sit down, son, and tell us what Audrey could possibly have told the reporter to make her believe that Sabrina is a call girl," his father demanded.

Daniel sank into the leather couch, and his mother sat down beside him. His father remained standing, leaning back against his desk.

This was one conversation he'd hoped never to have with his parents. He'd promised Sabrina that they would never find out. But it was better his parents found out the truth rather than assume things even worse. Because Sabrina was no call girl.

"Tim and Holly really did set us up. That is the truth, but it didn't happen the way we told you."

"What do you mean?" Raffaela touched Daniel's forearm. He placed his hand over hers and squeezed it.

"As you know, right before I left for San Francisco, I caught Audrey in bed with Judd, my attorney. I broke it off with her right there and then. On my way to the airport I called Tim and asked him to . . . " He hesitated. Could anything be more embarrassing than having to admit to his parents that he wanted to hire an escort?

"You asked him to do what?" his mother asked.

"I asked him to find me an escort service."

"Oh, Danny!" His mother pressed her hand against her chest, clearly shocked. "An escort service? Why? You're better than that!"

"I know. But, I had a big reception to attend, and I didn't want to go alone. You both know how I hate those social events where every gold-digging socialite tries to dig her claws into me. And after what happened with Audrey, I didn't want to spend the evening fending off women like her. So, I hired an escort to go with me." He shoved his hand through his already messy hair. "I made it very clear to Tim that I only wanted her to pretend to be my girlfriend so that those single women at the reception stayed away from me."

"And Tim sent you Sabrina? You mean Sabrina really *was* an escort?" his father asked.

"Yes. No!" He stared into his parents' confused faces. "Tim sent me Sabrina, but she was pretending to be an escort. It's complicated." How could he tell the story without revealing that Holly was in fact an escort? He couldn't betray her confidence like that.

"I don't understand. Why would Sabrina pretend that she's an escort?"

"Tim first wanted to set me up on a blind date. I told him no blind dates. I was done with women for a while. I didn't want another messy relationship. So I guess Tim and Holly figured that they'd get me to go out with Sabrina nevertheless. So they concocted this whole elaborate scheme and told Sabrina to pretend to be an escort. But that it was really kind of a blind date." Well, it wasn't the entire truth, but it was close enough to the truth.

"I liked Sabrina from the moment I met her. Hell, I paid to see her again the next night. We fell in love." Daniel shook his head. "It was all very confusing at the beginning. But the point I'm trying to make here is that Sabrina is not a call girl. She never was."

"I'm not sure what to say." His father stood and went to the mini bar in the corner. He poured himself a drink and took a sip.

"I still don't understand how Audrey fits into all of this. Obviously this was a private arrangement between Tim and Holly. No escort agency was involved. They were just playing," Raffaela said, her forehead furrowed.

"Audrey didn't handle the breakup well. She convinced herself that I was going to take her back. So she showed up at my hotel room in San Francisco when Sabrina and I were . . . " He glanced at his father who seemed to understand instantly. He didn't have to spell it out. "I don't know how Audrey could have found out that Sabrina was pretending to be an escort. The only people who knew were Tim, Holly, Sabrina, and myself. She must have been suspicious when she found me and Sabrina together in the hotel room two days after our breakup. I guess she figured for me to find somebody so quickly, she would have to be a call girl."

Daniel huffed. "Hell, it's not the first time that she's tried to sabotage my relationship with Sabrina. Audrey is an insanely jealous woman and she can't accept the fact that I'm going to marry Sabrina. Audrey knows I'd never come back to her, so she's out for revenge. I don't know how she managed to convince the reporter of her lies, but she must have fabricated something. And I'm going to find out what it is."

"How are you going to do that?" his mother asked.

"I went to Audrey's apartment to confront her, but her housekeeper told me that Audrey left a couple of days ago, and she doesn't know where to or when she'll be back. But I'm going to find her."

"Even if you find Audrey, do you really think she'll just confess to lying?" his father asked.

"Of course not, but I'll find a way to force her to admit to her lies. In the meantime I'm going to threatened to sue the paper for libel. I've already spoken to my attorney on the drive home. He's contacting legal counsel at the *New York Times* and will be threatening them with a lawsuit."

"You realize that this will get messy, right? There will be no way to keep this from Sabrina," his father cautioned.

"Which is why I'm not going to pursue any lawsuit until after the wedding. And no one is going to tell her either," he said, looking first at his father then at his mother. "I don't want anything to ruin Sabrina's wedding day. She deserves a dream wedding. And I'm going to deliver it."

"Agreed. Sabrina doesn't need to know," his mother said with a nod. "Holly promised me to not tell her anything either."

"Holly knows about the article?" Daniel asked. "Shit." Not that he didn't trust Holly, because he did, but the more people knew the more likely it was that somebody would slip up.

"She was with me when Linda alerted me to the article."

His father placed a gentle, reassuring hand on Daniel's shoulder. "I'm sorry we jumped to conclusions about Sabrina. We'll do whatever we can to make sure she doesn't find out."

"With Linda knowing about the article, soon all of the Hamptons will know, even those who don't read the *New York Times*. Do you know what that means? Your reputation, Dad," Daniel prompted, looking up at him.

"What about my reputation?"

"This scandal will rub off on you and Mom. Your reputation—"

"—can withstand the storm," his father claimed.

His mother smiled up at her husband. "This wedding will come off as planned and everything will be perfect."

Daniel smiled, more for his mother's benefit than his own. He just hoped she was right, because not marrying Sabrina wasn't an option.

6

"Is it just me or does it seem like today went on forever?" Sabrina asked as she climbed into bed next to Daniel.

He reached out and draped his arm across her stomach, pulling her tight to his body. Sabrina sighed when he nuzzled his face against her neck.

"It did go on forever." He kissed her neck, making her shiver pleasantly despite the warmth in the room. "And I know why."

"Tell me."

Against her back she felt his chest and bare stomach. Like always, Daniel slept in the nude.

"It's because we spent the day apart."

"Did you take care of everything you needed to in New York today?" she asked.

He nodded and brought his mouth to her neck again, pressing a soft kiss onto it. "I've done as much as I could." Then he sighed. "How was your day?"

"I went over the music arrangements with the pianist. I think we've covered everything. I wish you could have been there. He had some wonderful suggestions, and at times I had a hard time deciding."

Daniel brushed a strand of her hair behind her shoulder. His fingers grazed over her skin, then gently stroked down her arm to her elbow and forearm until she felt his fingers lace with hers.

"I'm sorry I wasn't there to help. But I'll help you with anything you want tomorrow."

"You're so sweet! But tomorrow I have the dress fitting with Holly, and I'm afraid you can't come to that, and afterward I'll have to go and find a present for Holly. Without her. So maybe you and Tim can entertain her while I go shopping?"

"A present for Holly?"

"Yes, it's customary for the bride to give her bridesmaid a gift. Don't you know anything about weddings?" She chuckled and turned onto her back to look at him.

He made a comical face and threw up one hand. "Hey, it's my first!"

Sabrina slapped a playful hand against his chest, laughing. "And it had better be your last too!"

His eyes twinkled. "I promise!"

Her heart skipped a beat and her laughing subsided when she noticed the heated desire in his eyes. She'd never before in her life felt so loved.

"I love you," he murmured, his face serious all of a sudden, his eyes locking with hers as if he wanted to tell her something important. "It would kill me if I lost you."

At his strange words she felt her forehead furrow. "Why would you lose me?"

His hand came up to cup her nape, his thumb stroking over her cheek as he bent over her, shifting his body so he was hovering over her. "I need you so much."

Then his lips were on hers, claiming her as if he were a conqueror who took possession of a new continent, intent on making it his. His tongue foraged into her mouth, kissing her so hard and so deep that she wondered if she would ever recover from it. She'd always loved the way he kissed her: with single-minded determination, with passion and an eagerness that was unparalleled.

But tonight he topped even that.

There was nothing frantic in his movements, nothing hurried. Yet at the same time his kiss was urgent and all-consuming. Deliberate, as if he had something to prove.

And just like his lips and his tongue fueled the fire in her body, his hands weren't idle and contributed to the sizzling flames that engulfed her body and threatened to incinerate her if Daniel didn't drive his cock into her soon.

When his thumb slipped underneath her negligee and rubbed across her nipple, she cried out, unable to contain the sensations that raced through her.

"You like that, don't you?" he teased before lowering his head and simultaneously pushing one spaghetti strap off her shoulder to free one breast.

She gasped with pleasure when his tongue licked around her nipple and his mouth enveloped it.

"Yes, I love it," she hummed and thrust her breast deeper into his mouth.

A low, animalistic groan bounced against her nipple.

Sabrina looked down at Daniel's dark head of hair, in awe of how he lavished so much care on her. Sabrina threaded her fingers through his hair and arched into him. She loved how he suckled her breasts.

"More," she moaned softly.

In response to her demand, his hands divested her of her negligee and tossed the garment to the foot of the bed. Now she was naked like Daniel. Bare in front of him.

When he lifted his head from her breast, she noticed the way he looked at her: hot, feral, lustful, and at the same time full of affection.

"God, I'm one lucky son of a bitch."

His voice was different, too. It was raspy and filled with raging need. She loved hearing it, craved it in fact, and relished the knowledge that it was a voice reserved specifically for her, for when they were alone.

Sabrina watched him as he continued caressing and kissing her breasts. She loved seeing the subtle changes in his face as he touched her and made love to her. When she reached for him, trying to pull him up to her to feel his hard body on top of hers, he encircled her wrists and stopped her.

"Just lie back and let me love you tonight, baby."

She licked her lips and nodded, because she recognized the look on his face; it was one that brooked no refusal. He was determined to lavish her with pleasure tonight. With a sigh, she dropped her head back onto the pillow and gave herself over to him.

Daniel's descent on her body was slow and torturous as he kissed and licked and nibbled every inch of her bare skin.

When he reached her sex, he paused and took a deep breath, his eyes roaming over her. He took his time looking at her, almost as if he'd never before seen her like this: naked and aroused, yearning for his touch.

"What is it?" she asked self-consciously.

"I have to memorize you like this."

"Why?" she murmured.

"I don't know. I just know that I have to. There's something different about you tonight." He smiled softly.

Sabrina swallowed hard. He thought her to be different tonight? Did he suspect something? Did he sense the change in her that she'd started sensing?

But she had no time to dwell on it, because Daniel lowered his head to her sex.

When his lips touched her and his tongue lapped at her drenched folds, she closed her eyes and pressed her head harder into the pillow, while her hips involuntarily jerked toward him. Daniel spread her thighs wider, his fingers stroking along her cleft, while his tongue licked over her clit, igniting her.

Her heart beat violently, her breaths came in shallow pants, and her hands grabbed the bed sheet for support, clasping the luxurious fabric in her palms to force herself not to lift off the bed.

"Oh God!" she choked out.

Daniel knew how to pleasure a woman. He never failed to arouse her and drive her wild. With every lick and stroke, he drove her closer to the point of no return. Lust and pleasure spiraled higher, making her body perspire and her heart pound like a drum. She writhed underneath his mouth, but his hands clamped over her thighs, preventing her from moving. She was at his mercy, vulnerable, yet safe.

"So close," she whispered. "I want you inside me."

Daniel's head reared up, and cool air wafted against her burning sex. Her entire body tingled. As he shifted and brought his body over hers, positioning his cock at her core, she reached down to him, wanting to feel his rock-hard shaft in her hand. But Daniel jerked his hips back.

"Don't touch me, Sabrina," he said gruffly.

For a fleeting moment, she pulled back, stunned.

"I'm sorry, baby," he said quickly, his eyes looking at her apologetically. "But I'm barely holding on by a thread, and if you touch me now, it'll be over before it begins."

She lowered her lids seductively. "Then start," she urged him on.

Sucking in a breath, she held it as Daniel thrust into her. A slow delicious burn spread through her body as it stretched to welcome him. He filled her so completely, it was as if they were one being, their bodies perfectly in synch, their hearts beating as one.

"I need you, Daniel."

"And I need you more than you can know."

Daniel slowly withdrew and then plunged all the way back in, this time even harder, deeper than before.

Sabrina wrapped her legs around him, holding him to her, not wanting to ever let him go. Like a couple that had danced together for decades, their bodies moved in perfect harmony, coming together, then separating, then joining again. It was a symphony of love, of lust and passion.

When Daniel pressed his lips onto hers and took her mouth for a searing kiss, Sabrina felt as if she were lifted in the air, floating on a cloud. Everything around them melted into the distance and became a blur. Only the two of them counted. Only the two of them existed in that moment.

Sabrina arched beneath him, lifting her hips to meet his continued thrusts, wanting more, needing more of him, of his cock.

He ripped his lips from hers. "I could stay inside you forever."

Forever. That single word swirled around her like an added caress.

Daniel dropped his forehead to hers and closed his eyes. His jaw clenched. "But I can't hold it back any longer. I'm gonna . . . oh baby, I'm gonna come. I'm sorry."

His thrusts became hard, fast, and frantic. He was losing control, and she loved every second of it, because she was the reason for it. The reason his face was contorted with pleasure, the reason he couldn't stop moving inside of her, and the reason his breaths were short and ragged.

Inside her, she felt his cock jerk. It made her muscles clench around him. Her legs tightened around his backside, and she let herself go, welcoming the waves of pleasure that raced through her.

"Daniel," she moaned as her orgasm claimed her. "Oh, God, Daniel . . . " Her words trailed into a soft sigh as she surrendered fully to him.

Daniel clutched her shoulders as he thrust one more time, burying himself so deep that she cried out. She felt the warm spray of his semen fill her at the same time.

Moments later, he collapsed on top of her, braced on his elbows and knees, his face nuzzled against her neck. His hot breath tickled pleasantly. Breathing hard, Sabrina held him firmly, not wanting to ever let him go.

"Are you okay, baby?" he whispered against her neck.

"More than okay." She smiled. "Wow, you were different tonight."

He lifted his head and gazed into her eyes. "Different how?"

She cocked her head and studied him for a moment. "I don't know. More intense. Did something happen while you were in New York today?"

"No. Nothing happened. I just missed you." Then he took her mouth for another kiss, preventing her from speaking.

7

Sabrina came down the stairs and looked around. "Holly?" she called out.

"In the kitchen," her friend responded.

She walked toward the kitchen, entering it a moment later. "Are you ready for the dress fitting? We've gotta leave in a minute."

Holly put her finger over her lips to stop Sabrina from saying anything further and pointed to Raffaela who was talking on the phone. Her future mother-in-law appeared flustered.

"This is awfully short notice to be canceling. But fine. If you don't want to come to the wedding, then don't come. We don't need or want people like you here anyway." Raffaela huffed with disgust. "Well I'm glad you're not coming!" She slammed the receiver onto its cradle.

Sabrina glanced at Holly, tossing her a questioning look, but Holly simply shrugged, throwing her arms up in a helpless gesture.

"Good morning, Raffaela. What was that about?" Sabrina pointed to the telephone.

"Oh, nothing." Raffaela smiled sadly.

"Somebody canceled?" Sabrina pressed.

Raffaela sighed. "It's really no big deal, dear, please don't worry about it. Sometimes people just cancel last minute, because they can't keep their calendars straight."

"Are you sure? You sounded very upset. We're getting so close to the wedding and I want to make sure there will be no last minute problems to deal with."

"It's nothing that important. It's just upsetting when somebody who said weeks ago that they were coming cancels all of a sudden." Raffaela shrugged. "It's no big deal. These things just happen sometimes." She smiled and patted Sabrina's hand. Then she took a pen and crossed out a name on the guest list, before placing it back on the counter next to the phone.

Sabrina's gaze fell onto the list. She instantly noticed red lines going through several names on the list and picked up the piece of paper.

"What's this? I only printed the guest list out yesterday morning. Did all these people cancel since yesterday?" She counted down the list. "That's seven guests."

Raffaela took the list from her hands, a tight smile on her face. "Honestly, don't worry about it, *cara*. It's normal for that to happen. When I got married, half of my family canceled on me at the last minute."

Sabrina gasped. "But that's horrible. I'm so sorry that happened to you." She couldn't imagine not having family present at her wedding. Though she knew that making sure that no fight broke out between her mother and her father, who were divorced, would be an achievement worthy of a Nobel Peace Prize.

"Of course, this does throw the seating all out of whack." Raffaela frowned. "I'd better re-do the seating chart."

"Do you need some help with that?" Sabrina offered.

"No, I can handle it." Raffaela pointed to the car keys in Sabrina's hand. "Where are you off to?"

"Holly and I need to go to the dressmaker for a last fitting." Sabrina expectantly looked at her friend. "Are you ready?"

Holly nodded. "Let me just grab my handbag."

Moments later, Sabrina and Holly were sitting in Daniel's sports car and driving the short distance toward downtown Montauk, where the seamstress was working out of a tiny bridal boutique.

"I love this car," Holly said. "I'm surprised Daniel let's you borrow it. What's he driving then today?"

Sabrina gave her a sideways glance. "He borrowed his dad's Mercedes and is running errands with Tim. I told him I'd drop you off at the Maidstone Country Club around lunch time before I go shopping in East Hampton, so you can have lunch with the guys."

"You're going shopping after the fitting? Why would you drop me off for lunch then? I don't need food as much as I need to go shopping."

Sabrina laughed. Of course Holly would react like that. "Sorry, honey, but that's one shopping trip I'll be making alone."

"But why?" Holly fidgeted in her seat.

"Don't ask."

"Come on," Holly insisted. "Why can't I come? You know how much I love shopping."

Sabrina sighed. "You can't come, because I'm buying a present for you."

"A present? For me?" Holly firmly jumped up and down in the passenger seat.

Sabrina laughed. "You're like a little child before Christmas!"

"Oh, you know how much I like presents. You're the sweetest friend ever!" Holly put her hand on Sabrina's forearm and squeezed. "I really don't deserve you!"

Sabrina chuckled. "Yes, you do. Without you, I wouldn't have met Daniel. And I wouldn't be as happy as I am now." At the words, she felt tears well up and pushed them back down. She was getting so sentimental lately. And this wasn't the first time in the last couple of weeks that she was getting teary-eyed without a reason.

"Yeah, that was quite something, wasn't it?" Holly turned her head and looked outside, but the sad sound in her friend's voice hadn't escaped Sabrina's attention.

"What's wrong?"

"I've been thinking a lot the last few days," Holly started.

"About what?"

"You, the wedding, your life. Happiness in general. You know."

"If you're thinking about happiness, then why do I get the impression that you're sad?" Sabrina took her eyes off the road for a moment and glanced at her friend.

Holly turned to face her. "I've been thinking about getting out of the escort business."

"Oh my god, really?" Equal measures of surprise and joy shot through Sabrina. While she'd never judged her friend because of her choice of occupation, she'd always secretly hoped that one day Holly would leave the world of escort services behind and start fresh.

Holly smiled a tentative smile. "I mean, it's just a thought. I don't really know yet how. I mean, I don't have that much money saved up, and I'm not really sure what else I can do, but I think it's time to change my life."

"Holly, that's great! I'm so happy for you. Not that I would have ever judged you, I mean—"

"I know that," Holly interrupted her. "That's why our friendship has lasted so long. But it's also because of you that I want out."

"Because of me?"

Holly nodded. "I see what you have. Happiness and a future with a man who truly loves you no matter what. I want that. I want a man like that. But what man would love me? You know." She shrugged.

Sabrina tried to protest, but Holly cut her off immediately.

"Don't. We both know it's the truth. No man can respect me if I continue to do what I do. It was fine for a while. It paid the bills. And there were times when I really enjoyed what I was doing. I don't regret it. But I want to move on now." She waved to the houses they passed along the highway. "I want this. I want a home, a husband, kids. I want to be respectable."

Sabrina gave her friend a warm smile. "And you'll get it. You will. Because I know you. Once you've set yourself a goal, you'll achieve it. You're strong. Stronger than I."

Holly chuckled. "I don't know about that. You're pretty strong. And resilient."

"So are you."

Sabrina slowed the car and set the blinker, turning at the next intersection. Half a block farther, she pulled to the curb and parked the car in front of a small store whose window displayed a seamstress's mannequin wearing a partially finished dress.

"We're here."

"This is not where you bought the wedding dress, right?" Holly asked.

"Of course not. But I didn't want to go back to New York for the fitting, so I found somebody local to make the final alterations. She's really good. Raffaela recommended her."

Sabrina got out of the car, and Holly did the same. Then they both walked to the entrance of the small store and opened the door. A bell tinkled as they entered and closed the door behind them.

"Ah, Sabrina!" the heavy-set woman greeted her, her eyes sparkling with motherly warmth. "And you brought a friend." She walked toward them with her hand stretched out.

Sabrina shook it. "Good morning, Julia! This is my friend Holly. She's my bridesmaid."

"Oh, so nice to meet you!"

"Nice to meet you, too," Holly responded.

"Well, let's get started then." The seamstress walked to the door, locked it from the inside, then pulled a shade down for privacy. Then she did the same with the window, before turning back to Sabrina and Holly.

"Let's get you into the dress and see what we need to do."

Swiftly and efficiently, Julia helped her get undressed, before helping her into the wedding dress.

"Step onto the podium," she instructed and pointed to a small wooden platform only about a foot higher than the floor.

Sabrina did as instructed.

"It's beautiful!" Holly exclaimed, looking at her with an open mouth. "Gorgeous! I know you emailed me a photo before, but it's even more beautiful with you wearing it. Perfect!"

Sabrina smiled. "I feel like a princess." She looked in the wall mirror at herself. The top of her dress was a bustier hugging her boobs, and at her waist, the silk fabric widened into a mass of cloth that made her feel like she was drowning in cotton candy.

"And you look like one," Julia added. "Now turn and let me see the length in the back."

Sabrina turned as if she were trying to make a pirouette on ice and instantly felt dizzy. She reached out her arms, trying to steady herself. Before she could fall, Holly had grabbed her arm and supported her.

"Are you okay?"

Sabrina took a deep breath and tried to regain her balance. "Just a little dizzy. Sorry. I shouldn't have moved so fast."

"Can I get you anything?" Julia asked, her voice laced with concern.

"Maybe just a glass of water."

"Of course." The seamstress disappeared into the back room.

"Are you sure you're okay?" Holly asked again, looking her up and down.

"Yes, I'm fine. It's just . . . " Sabrina hesitated, then lowered her voice to a whisper. "I think I'm pregnant."

"What?" Holly's eyes widened in surprise.

"Shhh!" Sabrina cautioned with a look to the door through which the seamstress had disappeared. "I took a home pregnancy test yesterday, and it was positive."

"Oh my god!" Holly cupped her hands over her mouth and shook her head. "Are you sure?"

Sabrina shrugged and brushed nervously over her gown's skirt. "I don't know. I only did the home test. With all the wedding preparations I don't have time to see a doctor. It will have to wait."

"But you have to see one, Sabrina. Like, today," Holly insisted. "If you want to, I'll come with you."

"Thanks, Holly, but I think I'll wait until after the wedding."

Holly tilted her head to the side, her look one of disapproval. "Why?"

"I'm stressed out enough as is, Holly. I don't need this looming over my head as well."

"Do you want this baby?"

"What? Of course I want it!" Sabrina cupped her hands protectively over her stomach. Having Daniel's baby would be a dream come true. Finding out before the wedding that the home pregnancy test was wrong would be a huge disappointment, one that she didn't want to face right now. "What kind of question was that?"

"An honest one." Holly placed her hands at her hips as if ready for a fight she was determined to win. "I just don't understand why you don't want to go to the doctor and find out for certain. It seems like not knowing would cause more stress than actually knowing." Holly frowned. "Have you told Daniel about this yet?"

Sabrina averted her gaze and shook her head.

"Sabrina! Why not? Are you afraid he'll be upset?" Holly asked.

"No, why would he be upset?" Sabrina asked quickly and adamantly. "I know he'll be thrilled, but I don't want to tell him until I'm one hundred percent sure. It would crush him if I told him I was pregnant, and then found out I wasn't. You know how inaccurate those home tests can be."

"Which is all the more reason to go see the doctor as soon as possible," Holly pressed.

"I'll think about it, okay?"

Holly nodded reluctantly.

"In the meantime, I need you to promise me that you won't say anything about this to anyone. Not even Tim."

Holly sighed. "Fine. My lips are sealed for the time being." Then she broke into a smile. "I can't believe you're going to have a baby."

"I know!" Sabrina squealed with delight and hugged Holly. "And you're going to be an aunt." Because to her, Holly was like the sister she never had.

"Oh, I'm going to be the best aunt in the world." Holly laughed.

"I have no doubt about it."

"I'm going to spoil that baby as if she were my own."

"She?" Sabrina laughed. "What makes you think it's a girl?"

Holly shrugged. "Women's intuition? Okay, so I'm hoping for a girl so I can show her how to shop and get her nails done and tell her all about boys."

Sabrina had to stop laughing and try to appear normal again when the door opened and Julia appeared with a glass of water. She didn't want anybody else to find out prematurely, because she knew just how fast gossip could spread in a small community like Montauk.

8

After dropping Holly off at the Maidstone Country Club, Sabrina drove into the village of East Hampton.

It looked busy in town when she arrived. Nevertheless, she found an empty parking spot and pulled in. After stuffing several coins into the meter, she adjusted her purse on her shoulder and walked along the sidewalk, not sure yet what she should get for Holly.

She wandered along the main street, glancing in store windows, trying to find inspiration, when she saw Mrs. Teller, the Sinclair's next door neighbor coming toward her.

"Hi, Mrs. Teller," she called out to her with a smile.

The woman's eyes widened, clearly recognizing her. But instead of returning Sabrina's friendly greeting, she dashed into the street and crossed to the other side of it, before Sabrina had reached her. Surprised at her odd behavior, Sabrina stopped for a moment. No, the behavior hadn't only been odd, it had been downright hostile if she'd interpreted the deep frown on Mrs. Teller's face and the sneer around her lips. As if she were appalled by what she'd seen.

Sabrina looked down at herself, wondering if something was amiss with her wardrobe, but she couldn't find anything dirty or torn that would warrant such a reaction. Despite the warm temperatures that had most of the vacationers in the Hamptons wearing shorts, Sabrina wore a colorful summer dress that neither showed too much cleavage nor was too short.

Shaking her head, Sabrina continued walking down the sidewalk and tried to put Mrs. Teller out of her mind. Maybe she was having a bad day and wasn't in the mood to talk to anybody.

For a moment, she gazed into the window of a lingerie store. *Lisette's* was stenciled over the window. Holly loved beautiful lingerie. It was part of who she was. Yet Sabrina hesitated. The revelation that Holly wanted to quit her job had come as a complete surprise. A welcome one, actually. But did this change who Holly was? Did this mean that suddenly, pretty lingerie wasn't one of her priorities anymore? Sabrina shook her head at her stupid thoughts. Holly was Holly. She was an extremely beautiful woman with long blonde locks, a gorgeous smile, and a figure any woman would kill for. Even if she didn't plan to work as an escort anymore, she would still take care of her appearance, and her taste in lingerie would certainly not change.

Having convinced herself that lingerie was always the perfect gift for her friend, she entered the store. A doorbell chimed and soft music played from speakers somewhere in the ceiling. Inside the store it smelled of scented candles. She'd been to this shop once before with Raffaela and found the sales staff very helpful, though she didn't think she really needed any help this time. She knew Holly's taste as well as her size.

One sales woman was busy helping another customer at a display of bras while the owner of the store stood at the checkout and finalized another customer's purchase. She looked up for a moment, glancing at Sabrina, a smile already on her lips, when her eyebrows snapped together and her lips set in a grim line.

"Hi," Sabrina said in her direction, but got no response.

Feeling awkward, she cast a look over her shoulder, checking whether anybody else had entered behind her who might have caused the scowl on the owner's face, but there was nobody.

Brushing off the feeling of unease, Sabrina walked to a display of negligees and browsed through the selection, gravitating toward items in black and red, two of Holly's favorite colors when it came to lingerie.

She lifted a red negligee with black trim made of lace and inspected it more closely. The fabric was soft, yet the lace felt rough and she wondered if it would feel comfortable on Holly's skin. Sabrina brought the lace to her cheek and rubbed it against her skin. And indeed it felt scratchy. Maybe she should get a negligee made entirely of silk instead.

She turned toward another display, when she nearly bumped into the owner of the store.

Jolting backwards, Sabrina gasped and pressed a hand against her chest. "Excuse me. I didn't see you."

The owner, Lisette, addressed her in a low voice. "I would like you to leave. Now. Without making a scene."

Shocked by her words, Sabrina's heart began to pound. Her eyes darted back to the negligees. Had she done anything wrong? "But I only touched the negligees."

"We don't want people like you here."

The hostility in the woman's words, made tears shoot into Sabrina's eyes. Why was this woman so nasty to her? She hadn't dirtied the negligee when pressing it to her cheek. Sabrina wasn't even wearing makeup that could have rubbed off on the garment.

"But—"

"Leave!"

This time the woman's voice was louder, and from the corner of her eye, Sabrina saw that the other sales woman and her customer had taken notice and were casting curious looks in her direction. The doorbell chimed again, and Sabrina didn't dare look in the direction of the door, not wanting for even more people to watch the embarrassing scene.

"What is going on here?" a familiar voice suddenly asked, making Sabrina look up.

Paul Gilbert walked toward them with long, determined steps, tossing the owner of the store a displeased look.

"Paul," she murmured, relieved to see a friendly face. "I think there's been some sort of misunderstanding. I didn't do anything wrong."

Paul nodded and placed a hand on her elbow, pulling her away. "We're leaving, Sabrina."

As he guided her toward the exit, Sabrina felt her control crumble and sensed tears running down her cheeks. When she was finally outside and Paul led her away from the store, her next breath left her chest as a sob.

Moments later, she felt Paul's arms around her, comforting her as she sobbed against his polo shirt.

"I only put the negligee against my cheek," she pressed out between sobs. "Just to see if the lace was scratchy."

"It's okay now." He patted her back as if she were a child.

"I'm not even wearing makeup. I didn't make it dirty." She pulled free of him and caught his confused look. "I mean no makeup could have rubbed onto the negligee," she explained.

Understanding shone from his eyes. "Forget about it. How about I buy you a nice cup of coffee?"

She sniffed and accepted the handkerchief he handed her. "Thank you." She lifted her head. "I'm not normally so emotional."

"That's quite all right. You have every right to be emotional. It's a lot to deal with."

She nodded. Weddings were stressful.

"Come, I know a great coffee shop."

Sabrina turned in the direction Paul indicated and froze. A few yards away, Linda Boyd stood watching them, her lips twisted into a sneer. That was all Sabrina needed now! Linda had seen her emotional outburst, and for all she knew she'd also watched the embarrassing scene in the shop. Knowing Linda, she'd probably stared through the shop's window.

Sabrina averted her gaze and forced a smile onto her face. "Yes, some coffee would be nice now."

9

"Well . . . " Father Vincent clapped his hands. "I think you two are ready for the big day." He smiled. "It will be a beautiful ceremony."

"Yes, it will be," Daniel agreed with a smile as he put his arm around Sabrina's waist and pulled her to him. "And we have you to thank for that."

"Oh, most definitely." Sabrina nodded. "Your introduction is lovely, Father."

"I'm glad you think so." He turned to Holly and Tim, shaking Holly's hand. "Well, it was nice meeting you both, too." He shook Tim's hand then looked back at Daniel and Sabrina. "If you two don't have any more questions or concerns, I'll be heading for my counseling session."

Daniel glanced at Sabrina, his heart swelling with love, and shook his head. "No, I think we're all set. Thank you again, Father, and we'll see you soon."

"Bless you." Father Vincent bowed slightly then left them standing in the aisle of the small church.

"Who's up for some lunch?" Daniel asked.

Holly wiped at her eyes and nodded. "Yeah, lunch sounds good."

"Are you crying?" Sabrina asked with a laugh. "Oh, Holly." She hugged her friend. "If it makes you feel any better, I'll probably be crying during the actual ceremony, too."

"I just can't believe that Tim and I actually managed to pull it off to get you two together," Holly said. "Maybe I should open a matchmaking business!"

Sabrina chuckled. "Maybe you should!"

Daniel laughed and started walking toward the exit. They really did have Tim and Holly to thank for all of this. If it hadn't been for them, he would have never met Sabrina and would have never experienced what true love was. "All right, let's go. There's a great little shack near the beach. It looks like a dive, but Frank makes the best clam chowder and crab sandwiches within fifty miles."

"Oh, you've taken me there before. Great place!" Tim agreed.

Daniel pushed open the heavy wooden door and squinted against the bright light of the midday sun. Behind him, the others exited, but before he could turn back to them and lead them in the direction of Frank's Crab Shack, an auburn mane across the street caught his eye.

He whirled his head to take a closer look and froze.

Audrey!

Audrey was just now entering the general store across the street, the door closing behind her. She was here in the Hamptons! Hiding from him in plain sight! So he'd guessed right: Audrey was staying close so she could watch with glee as chaos, caused by her vicious lies, ensued. She was most likely staying with the Boyds. No wonder Linda Boyd had known about the newspaper article so quickly and alerted his mother, when he doubted that Linda even read the *New York Times*.

His heart thundered in his ears, and his hands turned to fists. He would wring Audrey's pretty neck for the untruths she'd spread about Sabrina.

Daniel turned back to Sabrina and their friends. None of them seemed to have noticed Audrey enter the store. This was his chance, but he had to make it quick, before Audrey escaped him.

"Uh." Daniel cleared his throat. "Why don't you guys go on ahead and I'll meet you there?"

Sabrina gave him a confused look. "Why? I thought it was your idea to go to Frank's."

He pasted a charming smile onto his face, while inside he was seething. "If I tell you, I'll have to kill you." He winked playfully. Then he quickly added, "It won't take long. I promise."

Tim whistled, jabbing him in the side. "Sounds like Daniel wants to buy something special for you, Sabrina."

Daniel instantly noticed the smile that pulled at Sabrina's mouth. "Why didn't you say so immediately?" Her eyes sparkled.

He pressed a brief kiss on her mouth. "Looks like I can't keep any secrets from you."

"Looks like it." Sabrina winked and left with Tim and Holly.

Daniel waited and watched until Sabrina, Tim, and Holly were out of sight before he made his way across the street and entered the general store.

He surveyed the interior. A fair number of customers were shopping in the large store that carried everything from milk to greeting cards to glassware.

He spotted Audrey in the far corner looking at a display of fancy bottles of olive oil and balsamic vinegar. Quietly and swiftly, he approached her.

"Audrey," he said, coming up behind her.

She gasped and spun around to face him. "Daniel," she greeted him coolly, her eyes already darting past him as if looking for an escape route.

"We need to talk."

Daniel glanced around. Too many customers were close by and would be able to overhear their conversation, and what he had to say to Audrey wasn't meant for anybody else's ears.

"In private," he gritted out between clenched teeth, while his eyes searched for a place that would afford some modicum of privacy. A sign caught his attention.

Before she could protest, he grabbed Audrey's wrist and dragged her to a door. *Restrooms* was printed on it. He pushed the door open, pulling a reluctant Audrey with him, then opened the door to the men's room and pushed her inside.

"Get your fucking hands off of me!" she said, jerking her hand from his grasp.

Daniel locked the door. "I know it was you, Audrey."

"What are you talking about?" Audrey braced her hands at her hips and glared at him defiantly.

"Damn it, Audrey! Don't play stupid with me. It was you who went to the newspaper with that ridiculous story about Sabrina being a call girl. I know you were the reporter's source."

"Prove it!"

"I don't need to prove it. We both know it was you, so cut the crap!"

"So what? People have a right to know when somebody in their community brings a two-bit hooker into their midst and makes her out to be a respectable woman."

"Sabrina is not a hooker!" Daniel shouted and raised his fist. He'd never hit a woman, but by God, he was close to it now. "This afternoon, you'll be contacting the reporter, telling her that you made a mistake, that it was a case of mistaken identity and ask her to withdraw the story and issue an apology."

She smiled in the smug way that he'd always hated. "No."

"Don't push me, Audrey. You have no idea what I'm capable of."

"You're not the only one who can issue threats." She crossed her arms over her chest. "You can't order me around anymore! You dumped me for that lowly piece of—"

Daniel pushed her against the wall, pointing his finger in her face. "Don't finish that sentence!"

"Even if I don't say the word, it's still true. I have proof, Daniel! Hard evidence that can't be disputed. The paper won't issue a correction, let alone an apology. I have documentation."

"What fucking documentation? There is no proof, because Sabrina isn't a call girl! Whatever you have is faked!"

"It's not!" Audrey insisted. "I have it in black and white!"

"Tell me now, or—"

"Or what? I'm not your girlfriend anymore!"

"Thank God for that!" he muttered. He'd dodged a bullet when he'd found Audrey in bed with his attorney.

Audrey glared at him, her mouth now spewing venom. "I'm glad of it! Luckily I never married you! Imagine the horror of finding a charge for an escort service on your credit card statement! As your wife I would have sunk into the ground out of shame! Luckily I was spared that humiliation!"

"Credit card statement?" That's how she'd found out? He gripped her arms, leaning in so his face was only inches from hers. "How did you get my statements?" The only people who handled his credit card statements were his assistant Frances and himself. "Frances would have never—"

Audrey interrupted him with a laugh. "Wouldn't she? I think you forget who recommended Frances to you when you were looking for a new assistant."

Daniel released her as if he'd burned himself on a hot stove and stepped back. "Frances?" Fuck! How had he not seen that? How could he have missed it? It all made sense now: Frances had constantly kept Audrey apprised of his whereabouts, his comings and goings, even his purchases. And there had indeed been a charge from an escort service on his credit card statement.

And had Claire Heart told him the truth after all, that she'd contacted his office for comment, and had Frances claimed he didn't want to speak to her? Frances certainly hadn't passed Claire Heart's message along to him.

Audrey chuckled. "Yes, Frances helped me figure it out. I knew something was fishy when I surprised you and her that night in the hotel. I just couldn't put my finger on it. But when I heard about Sabrina's friend Holly, I remembered something: you'd called Sabrina 'Holly' that night. You didn't know her real name." Audrey straightened her blouse and smiled. "I put two and two together. And when I saw the charge on your credit card, I dug a little deeper. Honestly, in the end it was almost too easy. Sabrina is a prostitute, but she didn't even have the guts to use her own name. She used her friend's name, as if that would hide what she was!"

His blood ran cold. "You'll pay for this! Mark my words!" He unlocked the door and rushed outside, Audrey's mocking laughter chasing him.

When he reached the sidewalk, he took a few deep breaths. But they did nothing to tamp down his rage. He dug his cell phone from his pocket and dialed.

"Good afternoon, Mr. Sinclair," Frances answered the phone, clearly having recognized his cell phone number on her phone's display.

"You're fired, Frances! Clean out your desk and leave! I'm alerting security, and they will escort you out of the building."

A gasp came through the line. "Fired? But I don't—"

"Don't count on a reference from me! Maybe your friend Audrey can find you another position, but *I* don't employ people who are disloyal to me."

He hung up, for the first time in the last half hour feeling a flicker of satisfaction. Anybody who crossed him would meet the same fate as Frances. The newspaper would be next. And then Audrey would feel his wrath. But for that he needed to enlist help.

10

Daniel closed the door to the boat house and turned to face Tim and Holly.

"What's all this sneaking around about?" Tim asked.

"I don't want Sabrina to know what's going on." He looked at Holly. "Are you sure she's busy for the next hour?"

Holly nodded. "I've talked her into taking a long bubble bath. She needs it. She looks really exhausted. I think all that stress about the wedding preparations is getting to her. And yesterday when she got back from shopping for a present for me, she looked all agitated."

Daniel ran his hand through his hair. "Just another reason to make sure that she doesn't find out what's happening."

Tim raised an eyebrow. "Is this about the article in the *New York Times*?"

"You know about that?" Daniel asked, not even really surprised. He'd planned on telling Tim about it now, but was glad he didn't have to. He was aware that Holly already knew, because she'd been shopping with his mother when Linda had alerted them to the article—or rather when Linda had rubbed in the bad news with glee.

Tim motioned to Holly. "Holly told me."

Holly merely shrugged. "Hey, I just saved you the trouble. Besides, he knows the whole story anyway. So, no harm done."

"Just as well." Daniel sighed. "I know who's behind it."

"Who?" Holly looked at him expectantly.

"Who do you think? Audrey of course."

"Is that confirmed?" Tim asked.

"She admitted it. I went to the columnist who wrote the article and she claimed she had solid proof that Sabrina is a call girl, but she wouldn't give me her source or tell me what that proof was. I found out nevertheless and confronted Audrey."

"And? Is she going to get the paper to retract the story? It's clearly false. We all know that," Holly said.

Daniel huffed. "Of course not. We're talking about Audrey here. That's why we have to discredit the proof she has."

Tim braced his hands at his hips. "And what kind of proof does she have?"

"My credit card statement with the charge of the escort service. Though there's nothing in the name that suggests it's an escort service, somehow she figured it out."

"Fuck! How?" Tim asked.

"Most charges have a phone number next to them so you can dispute the charge if needed. I guess she called and figured it out somehow."

Holly glared at Tim. "See, I told you we should have never let it run through the agency!"

"He would have smelled a rat early on if we hadn't," Tim defended his action.

"Hey! Guys!" Daniel interrupted. "What's done is done."

"How did Audrey even get access to your credit card statement? Who did she sleep with this time?" Tim asked.

"She didn't have to sleep with anybody. She had my assistant Frances in her pocket."

"Crap!" Tim exclaimed.

"I fired her."

"Good for you!"

Holly leaned against a work bench. "Hold on, guys. How would she make the leap from a credit card charge by my agency to knowing that Sabrina was the one who showed up? Even if she was able to somehow convince the staff at the agency to release the name of the escort who took the booking, she would have gotten my name, not Sabrina's."

"Holly's got a point," Tim agreed.

Daniel rubbed his chin. "I'm not sure. She said she got suspicious, because I called Sabrina 'Holly' the night Audrey surprised us in the hotel room. So she believes that Sabrina used a nom-de-guerre, so to speak, when working for the agency. That she pretended to be somebody else." Which ironically was the truth. She had pretended to be Holly, but Sabrina was no escort.

"It shouldn't be too hard to disprove that. After all, the real Holly is right here." Tim pointed at Holly, who tilted her head sideways, glaring at him then lifting her middle finger in salute.

"No, Tim. I'm not going to expose to everybody what Holly does for a living. There has to be another way. Besides, then the rumor mill will really start to turn and people will assume I'm sleeping with Sabrina's best friend. In any case, I can't expose Holly."

Holly smiled at Daniel. "Thanks, it's good to know that at least one person here has some decency left."

Tim shrugged. "It was just a thought how we could play out a case of mistaken identity. Nothing personal, sweetheart."

Holly rolled her eyes then looked back at Daniel. "But you know I'll do it if that's the only way we can save the day. I will. But think for a moment. How can you mistake me with Sabrina or vice versa? We look nothing alike!"

"Well, so much for making a case of mistaken identity stick," Daniel said, resigned.

"Not so fast," Holly suggested.

Daniel stared at her in confusion. "What do you mean? I thought we just agreed that we won't tell them that you're the escort."

"Yes, we did. But I'm not talking about myself. If we want to convince the paper that this was a case of mistaken identity, then we'll have to give them a different Sabrina."

"I'm afraid I'm not following," Tim interrupted, rubbing his nape.

"So what exactly did you have in mind, Holly?" Daniel asked curiously.

She smiled mysteriously. "Let me work on it. It'll take a little time to set up, but I'm sure I can pull it off."

Daniel exchanged a look with Tim, who nodded. "Fine. In the meantime, Tim, can you find me a really good private investigator?" He knew that Tim's firm regularly used private investigators.

"Local?"

Daniel nodded.

"Sure can. I'll talk to my guy in San Francisco and have him recommend somebody in New York. What do you want him to do for you?"

"Dig up some dirt on Audrey. Nobody is squeaky clean. We need leverage to get her to go to the paper and admit that the documentation she provided is fake so that they will retract the story."

"Okay, I'm on it."

11

Sabrina stood on the front steps, a coffee mug in her hand, and watched the chaos unfolding in the driveway. Several trucks were parked there, and workers were unloading equipment in order to build a tent in the backyard, where the wedding ceremony and the reception would take place.

She bounced down the steps and weaved her way through the throng of workers, watching them with trepidation as they carried long poles toward the back of the house, trampling over Raffaela's pristine lawn, grazing her beautiful flowerbeds and destroying delicate plants with their boots.

Sabrina cringed, but she knew there was no other way to get to the backyard other than going through the house itself—which was definitely not an option. The workers would knock over priceless vases and other irreplaceable decorative items if they carried the poles through the hallway.

Sabrina turned, not wanting to watch the inevitable chaos any longer, when a FedEx van stopped at the end of the driveway. She waited until the driver jumped out and walked toward her, an envelope in hand.

"Good morning," she greeted the courier.

"Morning. I have a delivery for a Miss Sabrina Palmer," he replied.

"That's me." Sabrina smiled and took the letter he held out to her.

"Please sign here."

Sabrina placed the mug on the stone fence and scrawled her signature on the display window of the electronic device then handed it back to him. "Here you go."

"Have a nice day," he said and turned back to his van.

Curious, Sabrina ripped the envelope open. Inside was a single piece of paper. A letterhead from her current employer: Yellin, Vogel, and Winslow.

Her heart stopped. Once before, when she'd lived in San Francisco, she'd received a letter from her employer, also delivered by courier. It hadn't been good news back then, and she had the feeling that it wouldn't be good news now either.

Dear Ms. Palmer, it read.

This letter is to advise you that your employment with Yellin, Vogel, and Winslow is hereby terminated effective immediately.

You may collect your belongings at the front desk upon returning from your leave of absence.

It was signed by the office manager, not even by one of the partners.

Sabrina's heart raced. They were firing her? Without giving any reason? A sense of déjà vu hit her. Something was wrong, terribly wrong.

Tears burned her eyes as she reached for her cell phone. Surely this had to be some sort of mistake. She'd done nothing to warrant this. In fact, right before the leave of absence they had granted her to prepare for the wedding and go on a proper honeymoon, the partners had told her how well she was doing. Mrs. Vogel had even expressed her pleasure with Sabrina's performance on the job thus far.

She dialed.

"Law offices of Yellin, Vogel, and Winslow. How may I direct your call?"

"Hi Martha, this is Sabrina Palmer. May I please speak to one of the partners, whichever one is available, it doesn't really matter who," Sabrina said with impatience as she paced back and forth on the driveway.

There was a long pause on the other end of the line. "I'm sorry, Ms. Palmer, but the partners are tied up in a meeting and won't be available for most of the day."

It was a lie, and Sabrina knew it. She could hear it in the receptionist's voice. Not only had the partners fired her, they had instructed the receptionist not to put Sabrina's call through. What was going on?

"Thank you," she mumbled and hung up.

But they wouldn't be rid of her so quickly. She scrolled through the contact list and found the direct number to Celeste, Mrs. Vogel's assistant. She dialed it.

"Mrs. Vogel's office," Celeste answered on the second ring.

"Hello, Celeste. This is Sabrina Palmer. May I please speak to Mrs. Vogel?"

The quick intake of breath she heard coming through the line told her that Celeste was searching for an answer to her request. "Uh, I'm sorry, Sabrina, but she's out of the office. I don't expect her back until tomorrow."

Sabrina paused for a moment. The receptionist had said that all partners were in a meeting and now Celeste was telling her that Mrs. Vogel was out of the office.

"Celeste, please I need to speak to her. It's an emergency. I know she's there."

"I'm really sorry, Sabrina, but I can't put you through."

Sabrina fought back tears. "Celeste, please tell me what's going on. I just received a certified letter terminating my employment. I'm just trying to find out why. But nobody will talk to me."

Celeste hesitated, then lowered her voice to a level where Sabrina had to strain to hear her. "I'm sorry. We were all shocked when we heard about you being fired. But, you know, you can't really blame them."

"What do you mean? I didn't do anything! They praised my work before I left on vacation."

"It's not about your work." Celeste sighed. "It's about the article in the *New York Times* a few days ago. The one in the society pages. I'm sorry. I have to go."

The call was disconnected.

For a moment, Sabrina stood there, stunned. An article in the society pages of the *New York Times* had gotten her fired? With a racing heart, she ran into the house, realizing too late that she'd left her coffee mug on the stone fence, and rushed upstairs.

She reached the room she shared with Daniel a few moments later and snatched the laptop from the bedside table. She brought it to the little desk below the window and sat down. While the computer booted up, she nervously tapped her fingers on the wooden surface.

The moment her laptop was showing her the welcome screen and she had logged on, she opened the browser and typed in the website address of the *New York Times*. The site came up instantly. She didn't lose any time by scrolling through the stories, but used the search function instead, typing in her own name and hitting return.

The search results came back within a second.

She clicked on the first hyperlink. It brought her to the engagement announcement that had run several weeks earlier. Beneath a photo of her and Daniel, two paragraphs had been written about their upcoming nuptials. There was nothing incriminating in the article. In fact, her employers knew full well whom she was marrying: a business tycoon from an extremely wealthy and well-connected family in the Hamptons. They were also fully aware that Sabrina didn't need to work if she didn't want to. Yet, she didn't want to merely be Daniel's trophy wife. She'd insisted on getting a job where she felt she was contributing something. She had made it clear to her employers after the engagement had been announced that she intended to continue working after the wedding.

Sabrina clicked the back button and returned to the search results. She clicked on the second hyperlink. The same photo as before appeared and Sabrina was about to click the back button again, when her eyes fell on the headline: *Business Tycoon Daniel Sinclair to Marry High-class Call Girl.*

Her heart stopped for an agonizing moment. This couldn't be happening! But as her eyes flew over the text underneath the headline, dread and shame settled in her stomach.

A little birdie tells me that successful entrepreneur and millionaire Daniel Sinclair, whose equally wealthy family lives in Montauk, NY, has decided to marry outside his class. According to a reliable source, his fiancée, Sabrina Palmer, worked as a high-class escort in San Francisco, where she met Mr. Sinclair, who was a client of the escort service which employed Ms. Palmer. Neither Mr. Sinclair nor Ms. Palmer could be reached for comment.

Had somebody stumbled over the little white lie of being an escort that she'd told Daniel on the night they'd met, and thought it was true? The only other people besides Daniel and herself who knew about it were Holly and Tim. And Sabrina knew that neither of them would ever mention a single word about it to anybody. But who else? Could Hannigan somehow have found out after he'd surprised them at their little weekend getaway in Sonoma? She wouldn't put it past her former supervisor at her old law firm who'd so desperately wanted to get into her pants to make allegations like these if he suspected something. After all, he'd lost his job because of Daniel.

That anybody who'd done business with Daniel would do such a thing she doubted highly. Then she froze. Daniel! Once he found out, he would be enraged. And his parents, they'd be devastated. Clearly they didn't know; otherwise Sabrina would have seen their behavior change.

She glanced at the date of the article. It had appeared the day the newspaper hadn't shown up. Coincidence? She didn't want to speculate.

But she needed to speak to Daniel this instant.

In the kitchen, she found only Raffaela. Sabrina's stomach lurched at the thought of Daniel's mother reading the article. What would Raffaela think of her?

"Raffaela, have you seen Daniel?"

"He left about half an hour ago to go pick up the place cards from the printer. He'll be back soon." Raffaela smiled.

"Thanks. May I borrow your car?"

"Sure, *cara*. The keys are on the side table in the hallway."

As calmly as she could, Sabrina left the kitchen. Maybe it was best that she and Daniel had this conversation away from the house where his parents couldn't overhear them.

12

"Good afternoon, how may I help you?" the older, pudgy man said as he pushed his thick glasses back up his nose and stared directly at Daniel. His eyes looked huge behind the thick lenses, suggesting that his eyesight was extremely poor.

Mr. Peats of Peats' Printing was looking his age: at seventy-five he should be retired and taking it more slowly but Daniel knew from his mother that Peats' only son had never shown any interest in the business, and his grandchildren showed none either. Eventually, once Mr. Peats couldn't do the work anymore, another beloved local shop would disappear. It was sad, really.

"Daniel Sinclair." Though he'd known the shopkeeper for over thirty years, Daniel doubted that the man recognized him. "I'm here to pick up some wedding place cards I ordered a couple of weeks ago. I received a call that they were ready to be picked up."

"Ah yes. Of course." Mr. Peats nodded and shuffled through a stack of papers on the counter.

Daniel waited patiently, not wanting to cause the old man any stress while he searched for the correct order form.

Finally he pulled out a piece of paper and held it close to his eyes. "Ah yes, the Sinclair wedding. I've got it in the back."

He turned around and walked through the door behind the counter, closing it behind him.

Figuring that Mr. Peats would take a while, Daniel pulled his cell phone from his pocket and checked for any messages. After he'd fired Frances, he'd called a temp agency to fill the vacant position until he could hire a more permanent replacement. Though he had advised the temporary assistant that he was on vacation and should only be disturbed in absolute emergencies, he had received a few emails from her already, asking about how to handle various issues that had come up. Daniel scrolled through his messages, but there were no new ones.

Behind him, he heard the door open and glanced over his shoulder. He stilled.

"Eve?"

Eve McCall, his old high school girlfriend, breezed into the shop, wearing white Capri pants and a tank top that showed off her narrow waist and her perfect breasts.

"Daniel!" Her eyes widened in surprise and her face lit up as she walked toward him, smiling. "What a surprise!"

"I was just thinking the same thing. What're you doing here?"

"I had some business cards printed, and I'm here to pick them up."

Daniel cast a glance back to the door through which Mr. Peats had disappeared, hoping for the shop's owner to return soon. "Business cards?" he asked politely, though he wasn't really interested in Eve's answer.

"Yes, I'm starting my own little business."

"Congratulations! I hope it's a great success."

She didn't seem to mind that he didn't ask more details about her new business. "Thank you. And you, what are you here for?"

"Place cards for the wedding."

"Oh." Eve frowned then quickly pasted her smile back on her face, nodding sympathetically. "You're still going through with it then?"

Daniel sucked in a sharp breath. "Of course I am. Why wouldn't I?"

"Well, it's just, you know, after that article in the paper, I assumed that—"

"You assumed what, Eve?" he interrupted, though his voice remained even and calm. He wouldn't show her how the mentioning of the article riled him up. "That I wasn't going to marry Sabrina? She's the love of my life. Nothing will stop me from marrying her."

"I didn't mean to imply that you didn't love her. But I know you." She smiled sweetly, moving a little closer. "And I know that you don't tolerate that kind of behavior. Surely she must have tricked you."

Eve's saccharine-sweet voice started to grate on his nerves, but outwardly, he didn't show his agitation. "I assure you, Sabrina did not trick me. I know exactly who and what she is. And she's not a call girl."

"Oh?" Eve let out a snort. "Well, then let's just say for argument's sake she isn't, there are still plenty of people who think she is. I didn't think that was the kind of reputation you'd want your wife to have." She batted her eyelashes and looked at him innocently.

"What are you getting at?"

Eve reached out and touched his forearm. Though he'd enjoyed the ex-cheerleader's touch when they'd gone out in high school, he now wanted to throttle her for putting her hand on him.

"I'm just worried about you, Daniel. I know you're a very loyal person. We've known each other a long time. I'd hate to see you get hurt."

"I'm not going to get hurt." He stepped back, making her hand slide off his forearm.

Eve nodded. "Are you sure?"

He was saved from answering when Mr. Peats entered the store again, carrying a box. Daniel turned to him and pulled his wallet out of his pocket, while the old man placed the box on the counter.

"Found it. Sorry it took so long," he apologized and opened the box, motioning Daniel to take a closer look.

Daniel reached in and pulled out a place card, quickly inspecting it. "They look great." He was anxious to leave and get away from Eve.

"I'm glad you like them." Mr. Peats smiled broadly.

Daniel slid his credit card across the counter and watched impatiently while Mr. Peats swiped it on his card reader and typed in the amount.

"Please sign here."

Daniel hastily scrawled his signature onto the receipt, took his credit card, and grabbed the box from the counter. "Thank you."

He turned to leave. "Bye, Eve."

But Eve didn't give up so quickly. "Wait, I'll walk with you."

Not wanting to make a scene in front of Mr. Peats, Daniel didn't respond to her and continued walking to the door. When he opened it and exited to the sidewalk, Eve followed him. He turned halfway.

"I don't think you should make a hasty decision about this," Eve continued and put her hand on his free arm.

He wanted to remove her hand from his arm, but he was holding the box in his other hand.

"It's not a hasty decision," he pressed out from between clenched teeth.

Eve moved closer, leaning into him. "I still have feelings for you, Daniel."

Daniel tensed.

"If you're afraid that you'll be alone if you break up with her, don't be. I'm here if you need me. We were good together once. It could be like that again."

Before he could tell her that it would never happen, a shadow entered his peripheral vision.

"Daniel?"

Daniel jerked his head to the side. Sabrina had stopped only a few feet away from them. Her eyes darted to Eve, then Eve's hand, which still lay on his forearm. When Sabrina raised her eyes to meet his, he realized how this situation must look to her.

"Sabrina."

"We need to talk," was all Sabrina said in response.

13

Sabrina followed Daniel to his car and got in without saying a word. She looked out of the passenger side window while he drove north, her arms crossed over her chest.

Like a vulture, Eve McCall had already swooped in and was trying to snatch Daniel away from her. It was clear from the way Eve had glanced at Sabrina that she knew about the article and saw it as her chance to make Daniel change his mind about the wedding. Had she actually told Daniel about it? Did Daniel know or was he still in the dark about it? She couldn't tell from his reaction.

"I didn't know Eve was going to be there. She came in while I was waiting," he said long after they'd left East Hampton behind.

"I don't want to talk about Eve. I want to talk about us. In private."

She noticed Daniel nod and pull into a side street outside of town. The dirt road turning off the Old Montauk Highway led to a secluded beach framed by dunes. Daniel pulled the car to a stop and switched off the engine.

Without waiting for him to say anything, she opened the car door and got out. She needed fresh air. Daniel followed her as she walked down to the beach and stared out at the ocean.

She heard Daniel sigh behind her. "What's wrong, Sabrina?"

"Everything is wrong. The *New York Times* published an article about us, claiming I'm a high-class hooker." A sob tore from her chest. How would he take the news?

Daniel reached for her elbow and turned her to face him. "I'm sorry. I didn't want you to find out. I knew it would upset you."

"You knew about the article? When? When did you find out? Did Eve tell you when she came on to you just now?"

When he lowered his lids, she knew the truth. Disappointment coursed through her.

"I knew before today. I read the article the day it was published."

Sabrina pulled her elbow free of his grasp. "Why? Why would you hide that from me?" She turned her face away. "For the past few days people in town have been giving me strange looks. I couldn't figure out why. Now I know: they read the article. They think I'm a gold-digging prostitute who tricked you into marrying me!" She paused to take a deep breath. It did nothing to calm her.

"I'm sorry, baby. Ever since I read the article, I've been trying to get them to retract it and issue an apology. I was hoping that I could make it all go away, and you would never have to deal with it."

She shook her head. "Daniel, I got fired today!"

Daniel stared at her, stunned.

"The firm terminated my employment because of that article. Everybody thinks I'm a whore!"

Daniel gripped her biceps. "Don't say that word! That's not you! They're wrong. They're all wrong."

"Don't you see? It doesn't matter what the truth is! Because everybody believes the lies in that article. I can't make that go away." She tried to pull from his grip, but he didn't allow it.

"*I* will make it go away. It's my responsibility, because I am responsible for this."

She gave him an inquisitive look. "What do you mean you're responsible for it?"

Daniel released one of her arms and shoved a hand through his dark hair. "It's because of Audrey."

Sabrina's heart stopped only to restart at double the rate a moment later. Hadn't they laid their issues with Audrey to rest several months ago?

Daniel sighed. "She managed to get her hands on a copy of my credit card statement and saw the charge for the escort service on it. With it she concocted a story, and the newspaper believed her. I just have to discredit it."

"Hold it! How did she get your credit card statement?"

Daniel closed his eyes for a moment. "Frances, my assistant. Turns out, she was spying for Audrey all along. That's how she always knew what I was up to. I fired Frances immediately when I found out."

Sabrina pressed a hand to her chest. "Oh my god! Where is this gonna stop? How are we going to ever fix this?" She pushed back the tears that threatened to overwhelm her and rob her of her ability to think clearly.

Daniel lifted her chin with his fingers. "I'm already on it. I'm looking into a way to discredit her story. Please trust me."

"What are you trying to do?"

"Let me worry about that. You've got enough on your plate with the wedding preparations."

Sabrina looked at him and took a few breaths before she continued, "Daniel, we can't go on like this."

His face paled. "Like what?"

"You can't constantly keep things like this from me, Daniel. If this marriage has any chance of working, we have to be honest with each other, no matter what."

Daniel let out a ragged breath as if he'd expected a bombshell and instead only a small pebble had hit.

"You're right. I'm sorry. I'll do better in the future. I'll never hide anything else from you. I promise you." He lowered his head, his lips suddenly hovering over hers. "Forgive me? Please?"

It was impossible to reject his request. With a sigh she leaned toward him, brushing her lips over his and offering him the kiss he sought. When their mouths fused together, she felt his arms coming around her, cocooning her, protecting her.

Daniel lifted her into his arms then lowered himself to his knees, placing her with her back in the soft sand. Daniel's hand trailed down the length of her body until he reached the hem of her skirt, which he lifted just enough to slide his hand beneath it. His palm was hot on her stomach, igniting her with one touch.

He ripped his mouth from hers. "Do you think I'm crazy, because I want to make love to you right now?"

"Yes," Sabrina answered breathlessly as Daniel worked his lips along her jaw and down her neck. "But then we're both crazy."

He kissed her throat, before pushing her T-shirt up over her chest and pulling it over her head. "You are so beautiful, Sabrina," he said, gazing down at her, his eyes burning with lust.

Daniel leaned down, flicked his tongue over her lips, and then dove into her mouth again, kissing her hard and deep.

Daniel covered her with his body. "I can't wait to make you my wife."

He unhooked her bra and exposed her breasts to him. A warm afternoon breeze stiffened her nipples.

Her hands were already busy removing his polo shirt while her eyes cast glances to both sides of her, making sure they were truly alone. As far as her eyes could see, there were only dunes and sand and beyond, the waves of the ocean crashed against the shore. Their sound provided the backdrop to their intimate encounter, swallowing the soft sighs and moans as they tore their clothes from each other's bodies.

Daniel lifted her onto the makeshift bed he'd fashioned from their clothes and lowered himself over her, spreading her thighs wide, so he could slide between them.

His cock was hard and heavy, almost purple in color and curving upward. Sabrina reached for it, sliding her fingers over the velvet-soft tip and feeling it jerk under her gentle touch. At the same time she noticed Daniel clenching his jaw as if fighting an invisible enemy. That she could still do this to him—still bring him to the edge of his control—made her feel powerful.

"I want to feel you now," she murmured against his lips. "Take me."

The head of his cock breached her sex a moment later, making her hiss in a rapid breath, while her moist channel stretched to accommodate him. He slid inside her in one smooth move, seating himself balls-deep, his pelvis slamming against her forcefully. She tightened her legs around his back instinctively, not wanting to let him escape. But he pulled back nevertheless, sliding out of her almost all the way, before he thrust back in with even more force.

"Fuck, baby! Don't ever scare me like that again!" he ground out.

"Scare you?"

He delivered several hard and fast thrusts, clenching his jaw all the while. "Yes, you scared me. When you said we can't go on like this." He groaned, pulling his hips back. His cock plunged back into her as if to punish her. "I thought you . . . "

He didn't have to continue his sentence. She could see his thoughts in his eyes.

"I love you," she assured him.

"I love you, too," he murmured, before claiming her lips again and dueling with her tongue, thrusting into her mouth in the same rhythm as his cock did farther down.

Sabrina felt like floating on a bed of cotton balls as Daniel kissed her, while his hands roamed her body, caressing her, and his pelvis rocked against her, delivering thrust after thrust, his movements becoming more frantic with every second.

His moans were carried away by the ocean waves, which broke against the sandy shore and outlying rocks, just as her own sighs and sounds of pleasure were swallowed by the afternoon breeze that cooled them against the hot mid-afternoon sun.

Her entire body began to hum and tingle pleasantly. Her skin heated and her heart hammered against her ribcage in a rhythmic tattoo as if to pronounce the feelings it harbored inside it in Morse code.

With every thrust of Daniel's cock inside her, she felt her body tense, preparing for the inevitable. He'd never failed to pleasure her, nor did he now.

"Oh God, yes!" she cried out when the first wave of her orgasm crested and washed over her.

Then she felt Daniel's cock jerk inside her, and a moment later, his hot semen filled her, making his thrusts even smoother.

"Fuck!" he yelled out. Several more seconds, he thrust back and forth, until he finally stilled, bracing himself on his elbows and knees.

Ragged breaths blew against her collarbone, and she could feel his heart beat against her chest. For several minutes, they just lay there, the sun warming them, the ocean waves masking their heavy breathing.

After what seemed like an eternity, Daniel finally lifted his head.

"As much as I wish we could stay here forever, I think we should drive back to East Hampton, get your car, and drive home."

Sabrina opened her eyes only reluctantly, blinking against the sunlight. "Do we have to?"

Daniel kissed the tip of her nose. "Yes, we do."

14

Sabrina pulled into the broad driveway of the Sinclair's home and came to a stop next to a taxi. In the rearview mirror she saw Daniel parking behind her.

She jumped out of the car, when she saw a woman getting out of the taxi, while the taxi driver sauntered to the trunk to open it.

"Crap!" she hissed below her breath. How could she have missed her mother's arrival? Wasn't she supposed to arrive tomorrow?

Sabrina ran around the car, throwing her arms around her mother. "Mom!"

"Sabrina!"

When Sabrina released her mother, the scowl on her face had not yet faded. "I was waiting at the train station. Nobody came to pick me up."

"I'm so sorry, Mom! But I thought you were coming tomorrow."

From the corner of her eye, she saw Daniel walk up to them, but he didn't interrupt.

"I decided to come a day early so I wouldn't be too jetlagged. I texted you. I figured it's the easiest way to get ahold of you. You kids all text, don't you?"

"I'm so sorry, but I didn't get the text." Not that it would be an adequate defense when it came to her mother. She would let Sabrina feel her displeasure for quite some time.

Her mother huffed. "Well, I was lucky to find a taxi." She motioned to the taxi driver, who lifted her suitcase out of the trunk and shut it with a loud bang.

"Let me get the cab for you," Daniel offered quickly and pulled his wallet from his pocket to pay the taxi driver.

Her mother let her eyes run over Daniel for the first time. An approving smile spread on her lips. "Well, at least somebody here knows how to treat the mother of the bride."

Sabrina rolled her eyes. It appeared that Daniel had just passed Sabrina on her mother's list of favorite people. Luckily, Sabrina didn't care much. At least it would mean her mother would be appeased.

Daniel turned away from the taxi driver, who by the looks of it had received a generous tip, and put his wallet away.

"Mrs. Palmer, I'm Daniel, so nice to meet you." He stretched out his hand to greet Sabrina's mother.

"It's Thorson actually. I took my maiden name after the divorce. But call me Ilene."

"Ilene, we're so sorry that we missed your arrival. Cell phone reception can be a bit sketchy around here."

Daniel tossed Sabrina a conspiratorial look. Cell phone reception was perfectly adequate in the Hamptons. Sabrina smiled back. Daniel knew how to smooth-talk women, and it appeared that her mother had no defenses against his charm. Like mother like daughter.

"How was your trip?" Sabrina asked and reached for her hand luggage, while Daniel took the large suitcase, which appeared to contain not only the kitchen sink but also a ton of bricks if she interpreted Daniel's facial expression correctly.

"The flight was fine. But honestly, it's a hassle getting all the way out here from the airport. That train takes forever and stops at every hamlet."

"For your return flight, we'll drive you back to JFK," Daniel offered quickly. "I'm sorry we weren't able to arrange it this time, but there's been so much to arrange in the last few days. I just wanted to make sure everything is set for your daughter's perfect wedding."

Sabrina's mother chuckled, directing a coy smile at her future son-in-law. "Well, if you put it that way. Of course I want to make sure everything is perfect for my little Sabrina. Even if that means I'll have to take a backseat." She cast Sabrina a suffering look.

Sabrina bit her tongue. Her mother had never taken a backseat to anybody. And she wouldn't start now. "Thanks, mom," she said instead.

"Well, let's get you settled." Daniel motioned to the front door.

Before they reached it, a red convertible sports car pulled into the driveway, radio blaring. Everybody's head turned toward it. Sabrina recognized her father's dark head of hair immediately. Apparently he was still dying it, not being able to accept that he was going gray.

"Well, look at that," her mother said quietly. "It appears that your father is still in the throes of his midlife crisis."

Though her mother did have a point, Sabrina put her hand on her forearm. "Please be nice. I don't want any fight to break out at my wedding."

Outraged, her mother looked at her. "Don't tell me that! Tell him! He's the one who—"

"Please," Sabrina interrupted. "Just this once. After the wedding you can fight all you want. I promise, I won't interfere." She would be on her honeymoon with Daniel and not care about the rest of the world, at least not for those two weeks.

Pasting a smile on her face, Sabrina set the carry-on luggage on the ground and walked to her father, who'd gotten out of the car. He greeted her with open arms, pulling her into a tight embrace.

"Hey, my little girl! Look at you! You're all grown up now." He pressed a kiss on her forehead. "Now where's that man who's stealing you from me?"

"I believe you're talking about me, sir," Daniel's voice came from behind her.

"Nice to meet you, Daniel. I'm George."

As the two men shook hands, her father's gaze drifted past them and fell on her mother.

"I see your mother has already arrived." He nodded in her direction. "Ilene."

"George," her mother responded with the same icy voice her father had employed.

"Where's your luggage, George?" Daniel asked.

Her father turned toward the trunk of the sports car and opened it. "I've only got a small bag." He tossed a pointed look at the large suitcase and the carry-on luggage of his ex-wife. "I always travel light."

He lifted the bag out of the trunk and shut it. "But you know, if you don't have any space in the house for me, I'm fine staying at a bed and breakfast down the road. I drove by a few. I'm sure I'll find something."

"Out of the question, Dad!" Sabrina insisted. "Besides, the house has six bedrooms, so it's perfect. And it'll make everything so much easier with driving to and fro."

Her father smiled at her. "Well in that case, I don't think I can refuse."

Daniel motioned to the door. "Why don't we go find my parents? I know they're excited to meet both of you." He smiled encouragingly at Sabrina's mother and took her suitcase.

The front door was unlocked, and Daniel opened it and stepped inside, setting the luggage down in the foyer.

"Mom? Dad?" he called out toward the back of the house.

Sabrina entered with her mother, her father following them.

"Wow, what a huge house," her mother exclaimed, looking around in awe.

Sabrina had grown up middle class, and their house in Northern California had been very nice, but couldn't compete with the splendor of the Sinclair's house. Her parents' house had been a simple home; Daniel's parents' house was a mansion.

"Well, it looks like you're marrying better than I did," her mother remarked with a sideways glance to her ex-husband.

Sabrina was saved from commenting, when Raffaela and James appeared in the hallway.

"Oh my god!" Raffaela said, flustered. "We weren't expecting you today. I'm so sorry. I must have gotten the dates wrong." She wiped her hands on her apron and rushed toward Sabrina's mother. "You must be Ilene. The resemblance between you and your daughter is remarkable. And if I didn't know better, I'd say the two of you are sisters!"

Sabrina suppressed a chuckle when she exchanged a secretive glance with Daniel. Raffaela had a way of wrapping people around her little finger that melted all their defenses in an instant.

As their respective parents exchanged greetings, Daniel pulled her aside and wrapped his arm around her waist.

"Are we okay now?" he whispered into her ear.

She nodded, though she still had doubts. Everybody in the Hamptons knew about the article and thought her to be a call girl. How could she hide this from her parents? And while Daniel's parents seemed to have accepted his explanation, her own parents might not be as understanding.

She could only hope that Daniel's efforts to get the newspaper to retract the story and issue an apology would bear fruit. And fast. Preferably before the wedding. Or there would be no guests attending it.

Sabrina understood now why Raffaela was getting all these cancellations. Those guests had read the article and decided that they didn't want to be associated with the Sinclair family anymore. And the incident in the lingerie store that Paul had rescued her from? The owner of the store had wanted her to leave not because she'd rubbed her cheek against the merchandise, but because she didn't want a presumed call girl in her establishment. Sabrina was being shunned by the community that held the Sinclair family in such high regard.

Could she really do this to them? Go ahead with the wedding when it meant dragging their reputation into the mud?

Sabrina sighed and prayed silently that the story would be retracted swiftly and her reputation restored—and with it the reputation of her future in-laws. But if it didn't happen, she had a choice to make.

15

"You can do this," Holly encouraged her.

Sabrina took a deep breath and forced a smile on her face. She'd never been so nervous in her entire life. "There's so much happening right now. Maybe this is not the right time to find out."

Holly shook her head and opened the entrance door to the brick building, holding it open for her. "Don't stall. That's just nerves talking. Now, come, let's do this together."

Pushing her shoulders back, Sabrina nodded. "I can do this."

Then she walked inside and headed for the front desk, Holly by her side. "I'm Sabrina Palmer. I have a ten-thirty appointment with Dr. Chandra."

"Good morning, Miss Palmer. Your insurance card please."

Sabrina pulled her insurance card from her purse and handed it to the receptionist.

After the receptionist ticked a name off the list and ran her insurance card through her system, she reached for a clipboard, pinned two forms to it and handed it to Sabrina together with a pen. "Fill these out and bring them back when you're finished."

"Thanks." Sabrina took the clipboard and turned toward the waiting area.

Both she and Holly sat down. While Holly reached for a glossy magazine with celebrities on the cover, Sabrina filled out the questionnaire as thoroughly as she could. Then she handed it back to the receptionist and sat back down.

Holly closed the magazine and leaned closer. "So, what are you gonna name her?"

Sabrina glanced around, looking at the other women in the waiting room and found one of them looking at her. Did this woman recognize her from the picture in the newspaper? Had she read the article? Sabrina sighed. How could she think about babies and a future with Daniel right now when there was so much chaos in her world?

"We don't even know whether I'm pregnant," she responded under her breath and looked back at her friend. "It could all be a false alarm. It happens all the time; you miss a period, because you're under stress. And if anybody is under stress right now, then it's I."

Holly put a reassuring hand over hers. "Sweetheart, you need to learn to relax. Maybe I should take you to a spa for an afternoon."

Sabrina rolled her eyes. "I don't have time to relax. There's still so much to do. And now that my parents are here, I have to play referee on top of it. Besides, my mother is still miffed at me for forgetting her arrival day." She shook her head.

After consulting her cell phone, she'd had to admit that she'd indeed received her mother's text message apprising her of her earlier arrival. Sabrina must have simply forgotten it. Could this mean that she was really pregnant? She'd once read that a woman's short term memory suffered during pregnancy. And then there'd been the dizzy spells, and in the mornings she'd occasionally felt a little unwell. She wouldn't classify it as morning sickness, just a sensitive stomach.

"The way things are right now, I'm not sure I'm ready to be a mother."

Holly chuckled and shook her blonde locks. "You'll do fine, and you know it."

"Still, maybe this is not the best time." Their gazes locked. "You know."

Holly nodded.

Sabrina had had a talk with Holly the day she'd found out about the article, after Daniel had told her on the way home from the beach that both Tim and Holly knew about the article. After digging deeper, Daniel had also confessed that his parents were aware of the situation, but that he hadn't told them the whole story. And once Sabrina had heard the sanitized version Daniel had dished up to his parents, she felt a tiny bit better. At least Daniel's parents weren't horrified. They actually thought that the way Tim and Holly had set up their blind date was cute, despite the fact that it was unorthodox. If only they knew the truth!

"Don't worry, we've got it under control," Holly assured her, leaning closer. "Tim, Daniel and I are working on a few things. Give it another day or two, and we'll get the newspaper to retract the story and issue an apology."

"Tell me what you're doing."

Holly shook her head, glancing around the waiting room, before looking back at Sabrina. "I can't. Please, you just have to trust us. I just don't want you to get all excited. You've got enough to worry about right now. Leave it up to the guys and me. We'll take care of it."

Sabrina couldn't keep the frown off her face. "I would be less stressed if I knew what you're trying to do. At least then I'd have some hope that this . . . this problem will go away. But just knowing that Audrey is behind all this makes me want to throw up."

Holly patted her hand. "That's just the morning sickness talking. Don't worry about Audrey. She'll get what she deserves. I'll guarantee it."

"Your word in God's ear!"

When the door suddenly opened and brought with it a fresh breeze from the outside, Sabrina turned her head. She was surprised to see a man enter the OBGYN clinic—alone. Had he been a FedEx or a UPS delivery man, it wouldn't have been unusual, but he wore an outfit that looked like he was about to go sailing.

He walked up to the reception desk and handed the receptionist a small gift bag, then talked to her in a low voice, too low for Sabrina to pick up the words. Though the blush on the receptionist's face suggested that he was flirting with her. When the phone rang, the girl reluctantly answered it, and the man turned around.

Sabrina's heart raced. She recognized the man immediately. It was Jay Bohannon, one of Daniel's friends and one of the members of the Eternal Bachelors Club from which Daniel would be kicked out on his wedding day. Like Daniel's other friends, he'd apparently driven down from New York a few days prior to the wedding.

Sabrina lowered her face and turned toward Holly, hoping that Jay wouldn't see her. She didn't want him to tell Daniel that he'd seen her at an OBGYN clinic, because even if it turned out that Sabrina was pregnant, she didn't want to tell Daniel until their wedding night.

Holly stared into Jay's direction, which wasn't a huge surprise: she liked good looking men like any other living, breathing young woman.

"Yum," Holly murmured under her breath.

"Don't look!" Sabrina whispered.

Holly whipped her head to her. "Why not?"

"Sabrina Palmer?" the receptionist suddenly called her name, before Sabrina could answer her friend's question.

Sabrina jumped up from her chair, her hands nervously brushing out the creases of her summer dress. Jay's gaze snapped to her, and his mouth twisted into a broad smile.

"Sabrina!" he greeted her, walking toward her.

Sabrina caught the other women staring at her. Great! Now not only would everybody know who she was and connect her to the article in the *New York Times*, but they would also gossip about her meeting a handsome man at a women's clinic. What else could go wrong?

"Hi, Jay," she said hesitantly, stretching out her hand, but instead of shaking her hand, Jay pulled her into a brief hug. Well, he was a Southerner and they had met once before at a birthday party in the city. She couldn't really push him away without making him think something was wrong.

"Fancy seeing you here," he said lightly, then winked. "Guess Daniel will have his hands full very soon."

"Uh . . . " Sabrina glanced to the physician's assistant who was waiting patiently at the door that led to the exam rooms.

Jay bent closer and winked at her. "Don't worry, Daniel won't hear it from me." Then he grinned. "That is, if you introduce me to your friend here." He motioned to Holly.

"Oh, Holly, this is Jay Bohannon, one of Daniel's friends. Jay, my friend Holly Foster. She'll be my bridesmaid."

"Splendid!" Jay bent down to take Holly's hand to press a kiss on it.

"Miss Parker?" the physician's assistant called out again.

"Excuse me, please."

With a last glance at Holly, Sabrina followed the girl and marched into the exam room she pointed out.

16

From the door to their en-suite bathroom, Sabrina watched as Daniel stepped out of the shower and reached for the towel. Drops of water were running down his hairless chest, traversing the ridges of his sculpted abdomen and disappearing in the dark thatch of hair that guarded his sex. Even in a relaxed state, his cock was magnificent. Her womb clenched at the thought of feeling him inside her. But this time the sensation was different. Because in her womb their child was growing. With their lovemaking they had created a new life.

When the physician had confirmed the pregnancy, she'd at first not known what to feel and how to react. But as the day had passed, she'd felt the joy about the news grow to monumental proportions. So much so that she wanted to shout it from the rooftops. But she wouldn't.

This was a piece of news to be treasured. She didn't want it to be tainted by the trouble the article in the newspaper had caused. No, this news deserved a platform of its own. She wanted to treat this as the gift it was. A gift for both her and Daniel. And there was one special time to share this gift with Daniel: on their wedding night. It would make everything perfect.

"What are you thinking of?" Daniel asked as he wrapped the towel around his lower half, depriving her of the sinful sight.

"Nothing."

He walked toward her. "It's your parents, isn't it?"

She shrugged, glad that he'd guessed wrong. "They are who they are."

"What went wrong between them?"

Sabrina smiled softly. "You mean what went right between them? Not a lot. I guess they had different ideas of what kind of life they wanted to lead. Mom always wanted to keep up with the Joneses. And Dad couldn't care less as long as he could hang out with his buddies on Friday night and watch football the entire weekend. Mom wanted more. She used to be a very affectionate woman when I was little. But Dad wasn't. He just wasn't the cuddly type. I think Mom craved physical closeness. And he couldn't give it to her. He wasn't very demonstrative with his feelings. Don't get me wrong; they must have had sex. After all, they had me."

Daniel brushed his knuckles over her cheek. "It's sad to see how things can go wrong between two people who once loved each other. They did love each other once, didn't they?"

"I would hope so, but I don't remember ever seeing or feeling it. All I remember from my childhood were their fights, their sniping, my mother's tears, and my father's silence. Maybe they loved each other at the very beginning, before they had me. But I guess it wasn't enough. They just weren't meant for each other."

"Not like we are." Daniel pressed a tender kiss on her lips.

She reached for his hand, intertwining her fingers with his. "Yes, not like you and I. Still, I'm worried sometimes. My parents must have thought too that they were meant for each other when they got married. When they were in love."

"You shouldn't worry. You and I, we have a special connection." He took her hand and pressed it against the spot where his heart beat against his ribcage. "I can feel it. Without you, I don't feel complete. I'd always thought I didn't need anybody. But I do. I need you. And the last few days have shown me that when somebody hurts you, it hurts me just the same. I feel it physically."

Sabrina slid her hand that lay on his heart farther up until it reached his nape. She pulled him closer. "I've never felt as loved as I feel now."

"That must be because I love you more than anybody else ever could. You're everything I ever dreamed of, Sabrina." He sighed. "And if I didn't have to go to this darn bachelor party, I'd show you."

She smiled, brushing her lips against his. "Nobody will mind if you're a few minutes late." She kissed him softly, but before he could respond to her and deepen the kiss, she pulled back.

A disappointed groan came over his lips, and his hands reached for her, trying to drag her back. But Sabrina had other ideas.

She dropped to her knees and tore on the towel around Daniel's hips, jerking it off him and tossing it to the ground.

"Oh God! Baby!" he let out on a ragged breath when he seemed to realize what she was planning.

She stroked over his cock and felt it jerk. She noticed that with every second that passed, it grew bigger. More blood coursed into it.

Sabrina placed her hands on his thighs and pressed him against the wall behind him. Daniel groaned, and Sabrina couldn't help but smile. She loved it when he lost control. And Daniel was about to lose control.

Her hand wrapped around his now fully erect shaft, and she brought her mouth to it. Her tongue snaked out and licked over the mushroomed head as if she were licking an ice cream cone, though no ice cream flavor could be as delicious as the taste of Daniel's freshly showered body.

Feeling the hard flesh as she slowly descended on it and took him into her mouth, was a sensation she loved. It made her feel strong and powerful to bring a man like Daniel to his knees. She shivered when his hands touched her bare shoulders and brushed the spaghetti straps of her top off her shoulders, making it slide down to her waist. Cool air wafted against her naked breasts, adding to the erotic sensations that coursed through her body as she sucked Daniel's shaft longingly.

His hips rocked against her, gently at first, but with every thrust his movements became more pronounced. She took him deeper, while licking her tongue along the underside of his aroused flesh.

"Fuck, baby!" he ground out, his voice nearly unrecognizable.

Sabrina slipped one hand to his balls, cupping them. His hips jerked at the touch, and a ragged breath tore from his mouth, echoing against the tiled walls of the bathroom. She gently played with the precious stones and felt the sac contract under her touch, pulling up toward his impossibly hard shaft, which she gripped at the base to add more pressure to her sucking motions.

She felt him tense under her ministrations. Then she gently scraped against his scrotum with her fingernails. His cock jerked in her mouth.

"I'm coming! Fuck, I'm coming!" he groaned and pushed her back.

His cock slipped out of her mouth just as semen spurted from its tip, raining over her hand and his stomach.

Uneven breaths filled the silence in the room as Sabrina tenderly continued to caress his cock and balls.

When she looked up at him, she met his dark eyes and noticed the stormy look in them.

"If I didn't have to go to this damn bachelor party, I'd bend you over the nearest armchair and fuck you until neither of us could move a limb."

"That's sounds very naughty."

He breathed heavily. "Yes, because that's what you deserve for seducing me like this. And you know how much I like to dole out punishment, don't you?"

A bolt of adrenaline shot through her, fanning the flames inside her once more. "Not as much as I like to receive it."

17

"The extraordinary meeting of the Eternal Bachelors Club is now in session," Zach Ivers announced.

Everybody was assembled in Zach's *man cave* on the first floor of his weekend home in Bridgehampton, several miles south of East Hampton. His main residence was a swanky penthouse in Manhattan, but in the summer and on weekends, Zach liked to withdraw to this almost modest three-bedroom house on Long Island. Daniel could understand why: the house was right on the beach and had the most magnificent view of the ocean. Tranquility radiated from the house and its surroundings. Even now, in the dark, there was something peaceful about the place.

"This isn't exactly how I imagined my bachelor party," Daniel said, looking at the faces of the other seven members of the club: Zach, who presided over the meeting; Paul Gilbert; Jay Bohannon; Michael Clarkson, who was the treasurer; Xavier Eamon; Hunter Hamilton; and Wade Williams, all tall, dark and handsome in their own right. They'd all attended Princeton together, where they'd formed the club after a night of heavy drinking.

Hunter grinned. "You know the rules."

Wade jabbed Hunter in the side. "I don't think Daniel cares much about the rules."

"Guys, be nice!" Tim chastised.

"Tim, you've got no say, since you're not a member of the club. We're letting you stay for the meeting out of courtesy," Michael protested.

Tim braced his hands at his hips. "Which it totally outrageous. I should be a member. I'm a bachelor, just like the rest of you. The fact that I'm gay should not have any bearing on this."

Xavier and Wade exchanged a look then Xavier said, "Yes, but we didn't want anybody in the club who has an unfair advantage over the rest of us."

"Unfair advantage, bullshit!" Tim shook his head. "According to California law I can get married just like the rest of you."

"That's true. But that wasn't the case when the club was formed," Zach interjected. "So, sorry, Tim, but you can't join now."

"It just wouldn't be fair," Michael added. "After all, we all contributed money to the club's coffers for years, and to have you join without a buy-in wouldn't be right."

Tim rolled his eyes. "How much are we talking about then?"

Michael glanced at Zach who nodded. "Well, might as well get on with the treasurer's report." He looked down at his notes. "Last quarter we closed out at 3.72 million dollars."

Tim whistled through his teeth. "That's not exactly chump change."

Michael smiled. "Yes, and after Daniel's wedding in a few days, only seven bachelors remain eligible to win the money."

"Knock yourselves out, guys," Daniel responded. "Not all the money in the world would make me change my mind about marrying Sabrina."

Zach cleared his throat. "Well, since we're on that subject." He glanced at the other men in the living room. "The guys and I have been talking while we were waiting for you and Tim."

Daniel tensed. Were they going to try to talk him out of marrying Sabrina because they believed the story in the *New York Times*?

Zach made a calming movement with his hand. "Before you say something, Daniel, let me speak for the club."

Daniel leaned back in his armchair.

"We've all seen the article. We've known you for a long time, and we know what kind of man you are. What this reporter claims is clearly a lie. We stand by you and Sabrina. So, if there's anything we can do to help you get this rectified, we'll do it. You can count on us."

Daniel let out the breath he'd been holding. "You guys. I don't know what to say." He looked at them as all nodded at him, underscoring Zach's words. "You would really do that?"

Wade chuckled and cut in. "Only to make sure you're really leaving the club, of course, but who cares about our motivation?"

Jay and Xavier laughed at Wade's words.

"Obviously Wade is in desperate need of funds, which means he'll do anything to eliminate members from this club," Xavier explained.

Daniel couldn't help but join in the laughter. Their heartfelt offer to help had touched his heart, but he couldn't accept their offer. It would mean telling them the truth, and he had no right to expose Sabrina like that, or Holly for that matter.

"Anything for you and the lovely Sabrina," Paul said. "How is she doing?"

Daniel nodded at Paul. "Fine under the circumstances." Then he looked back at the others. "Thanks guys, but Tim and I have got it under control. I'm confident that the paper will retract the story shortly and issue an apology. They only have fabricated evidence which they have completely misinterpreted. It's only a matter of time until we've picked it apart and proven how wrong they are."

Despite his confident words, Daniel didn't feel as certain as he'd let on. With every passing day, it seemed more unlikely that they could ever convince the newspaper to retract the story.

He'd heard back from Elliott, his attorney, who'd reported that while he'd spoken to the legal counsel of the *New York Times* and threatened them with a law suit, they remained firm and were sticking to their guns.

And though Tim had hired a private investigator to dig into Audrey's life to unearth any skeletons in her closet with which to pressure her to retract her accusations, it was too early to expect any results from him. Which only left Holly, who was still trying to figure out how to make a case of mistaken identity stick.

"Well, in that case, let's get on with business," Zach said. "We've prepared your resignation papers which will become effective on the day of your wedding. Are you willing to resign from the club?"

Daniel nodded. "Yes."

Zach held a pen out to him. "Then sign here and we'll record it in the club's minutes."

Daniel rose and walked to him. He took the pen and signed his name on the piece of paper.

"I must say, Daniel, I've never seen a man who's signed away nearly four million dollars do it with such a happy smile on his face."

Daniel chuckled. "Once you find the right woman, you'll do the same."

"I won't give up that easily," Zach answered. "You know how much I love a challenge."

Behind him, the others laughed.

"Time to get the party started," Hunter announced. "So, when's the stripper coming?"

Daniel whirled around to Hunter, annoyance forming in his gut. "You've gotta be kidding me. I said no strippers."

Hunter boxed Wade in his side. "Told you he's totally pussy-whipped. The best stripper in the world isn't gonna do it for him. So, you my friend, lost your bet." He held his flat palm out to Wade. "That's a hundred bucks, please."

"Not so fast!" Wade protested. "Let's wait until the stripper is here."

"I canceled her," Hunter confessed.

Wade grinned. "I know. That's why I booked another one."

Daniel rolled his eyes. It appeared that there was no way to escape the obligatory stripper at his bachelor party. Well, he could at least let his friends have some fun.

He exchanged a look with Tim, who shrugged and said, "It's going to be as boring for you as it is for me. We might as well get drunk instead."

Daniel laughed. "You could always call a male stripper."

"And have the guys toss me out on my ass? No way, I'm not going to miss your bachelor party, no matter how little interest I have in a female stripper."

"In that case, get us some drinks!"

18

"You didn't have to go through so much trouble for us, Raffaela," Sabrina's mother gushed as she looked at the beautifully set dinner table. "We could have easily gone out for dinner somewhere."

Raffaela smiled back at her and put a hand on her arm. "It's a pleasure, Ilene. I love to cook for a large crowd."

While Sabrina knew it was true, she also knew that Raffaela had insisted on this dinner at home in order to avoid Sabrina's parents running into anybody in the village who might mention the *New York Times* article. The more time her father and mother spent at the Sinclair's house, the less likely it was that they'd stumble over the news.

"Well, that's refreshing: a woman who likes to cook," her father threw in, tossing his ex-wife a pointed look.

It had always been a bone of contention between her parents that her mother wasn't an enthusiastic cook.

"Well, it didn't help that you only liked hamburgers and steaks. What's interesting about cooking those?" Sabrina's mother retorted.

Before her father could respond, James interrupted, "George, why don't you sit to my right? Then we'll have a chance to talk a little more during dinner. I'm eager to talk to you about going out on the boat."

Sabrina threw her future father-in-law a thankful look. He winked back at her and took his seat at the head of the table.

Her father sat down next to him. Knowing that her mother didn't want to be near him, nor have to look directly at him, she motioned to a chair at the other end of the table, facing Daniel's father.

"Mom, why don't you take this seat?"

Sabrina exchanged a quick look with Holly, who sat down next to Sabrina's father to create an adequate buffer, while Sabrina and Raffaela sat down opposite them.

With Daniel and Tim having left for the bachelor party, the chairs had been spaced farther apart and the two spare chairs had been removed so that it didn't look like somebody was missing.

"I hope you all like veal," Raffaela announced.

"Mmm!" her husband exclaimed, then motioned to Sabrina's father. "My wife's veal piccata is to die for. Make sure you fill your plate quickly, or there won't be any left."

Raffaela actually blushed at her husband's compliment. "Ah, James, just because you like it, doesn't mean everybody else does." She tossed a look to the other dinner guests. "If you don't like veal or would rather have something vegetarian, I also made eggplant parmesan." She pointed to a casserole dish in the middle of the table.

Sabrina's father speared his fork into a piece of veal and lifted it onto his plate. "Veal is fine for me. I eat more than just burgers and steaks." He smiled at Raffaela, but Sabrina hadn't missed the backhanded comment directed at her mother.

"Well, help yourselves!" Raffaela encouraged everybody.

The clanging of dishes and cutlery bounced around the room, while everybody filled their plates with meat, vegetables, and other side dishes. Sabrina looked at Raffaela, who sat next to her, wanting to apologize for her parents' behavior, but didn't dare say anything in front of them. Her future mother-in-law seemed to read in her gaze what she wanted to say and smiled. "Don't worry, Sabrina. It's fine," she whispered.

"We have a boat out on the dock," James said, looking at Sabrina's father. "Maybe you and Ilene want to go out on the water tomorrow. I think I have a couple of hours, right, darling?" He smiled at his wife.

"If you think all the work with the tent is done, then I'm sure you have time, *caro*. I think it would be a great way of showing our guests the surroundings."

Sabrina noticed how her father glanced to the other end of the table as if trying to figure out what his ex-wife's reaction was. Sabrina's mother looked delighted.

"Oh that would be wonderful!" she said. "I've always liked boats. Of course, we could never afford our own." She tossed a disapproving look in the direction of Sabrina's father. "Even though we had the San Francisco Bay right at our doorstep."

Her father grunted and shoved a piece of meat into his mouth.

"Excellent!" James exclaimed. "How about you, George, do you want to join us for an hour or two sailing up and down the coast?"

"I don't think so. I'm not into fancy rich people's toys."

Sabrina gasped and dropped her fork onto her plate. "Dad!"

"What? Do you find me too ordinary for your new friends now?" He motioned to the richly decorated room around him, the elegant paintings on the walls and the expensive vases in the display cabinets. "Are you ashamed of the fact that I'm not as rich as your fiancé and his family?"

"Dad, don't!" She felt tears rise and pushed them down.

"Don't what? Say the truth?" He snorted and motioned to his ex-wife. "Has your mother finally managed to turn you into a mirror image of herself?"

"That's not true!" Sabrina said, raising her voice.

"Is it not? Look at you! You're all dolled up, wearing expensive clothes like the ones your mother always wanted to have but couldn't afford."

Her mother jumped up and tossed her napkin on the table. "Shut it, George! That's enough! There's nothing wrong with what Sabrina wears or what she wants. Nor the fact that she's marrying into a rich family. Just because you never made anything out of yourself, doesn't mean you can drag down your daughter with you!"

Her father pushed his chair back and rose abruptly. "You know what, Ilene? The reason I was never able to make anything out of myself is because you were hanging around my neck like a heavy chain that was dragging me down. So don't you criticize me! You lost that right when you divorced me!" Then he looked at Raffaela. "Thanks for the food. It was excellent."

Without another word he turned and left the room.

Sabrina couldn't suppress the tears any longer and felt them run down her burning cheeks. "I'm so sorry." How could her father embarrass her like this in front of her future in-laws? How could he be so cruel?

Suddenly, she felt Raffaela's soothing arm around her shoulders. "It's not your fault, *cara.*"

A moment later, her mother squeezed her hand. "Honey, don't take any notice of him. At least you're making a much better match than I did, and not even your father can take that away from you."

19

"Is Daniel not up yet?" Raffaela asked and opened the refrigerator to search for something.

Sabrina's father was sitting at the breakfast table, browsing through the paper, and her mother was pouring herself a second cup of coffee, but wasn't eating anything, which probably meant that whatever outfit she'd chosen for the wedding required her to shed another pound before it fit properly.

Sabrina smiled at her soon-to-be mother-in-law. "It looks like both he and Tim had too much to drink last night. Nobody was sober enough to drive. They're still at Zach's house."

Raffaela shook her head. "Oh, dear! Are you upset about that?"

"I don't have a problem with it. I would be very upset, though, if either one of them had been driving last night."

"Well, just a word of caution, Sabrina, and I'm speaking from personal experience," her mother interjected from the breakfast table. "It's a hangover here, an outing with his friends there, and suddenly your husband is never at home." She tossed a pointed look at her ex-husband.

A grunt came from him, then a muffled comment. "Some women just don't make it worth it for a man to stay at home."

Sabrina exchanged a look with Raffaela, who gave her an encouraging look and stroked over Sabrina's arm. Maybe having both her parents stay at the Sinclair's home hadn't been the best idea after all. She should have just told them to stay at a Bed and Breakfast.

Sabrina's mother huffed. "Oh, go ahead, read your outdated paper, and stay out of the conversation like you always do."

Her father lowered the paper and glared at his ex-wife. "At least an outdated paper isn't gonna talk back to me."

"You're reading an old paper? I thought I'd put them all into recycling." Raffaela asked.

Sabrina's father shrugged. "Found it under the seat cushion." With a sideways glance to his ex-wife he added, "Reading anything is better than having to talk to certain people."

Sabrina felt tears well up in her eyes again. She knew that the pregnancy was causing her to be so emotional about the smallest things. But her parents' sniping at each other didn't help. Raffaela looked at her, pity shining in her eyes. "Just a few more days," she whispered to Sabrina for only her to hear. A little louder, she addressed Sabrina's father. "I'm so sorry. I guess I forgot to bring in today's paper. I'd better get it now. James will want to read it too when he comes down."

Raffaela left the kitchen, and Sabrina could hear her heels click on the wooden floorboards as she walked toward the foyer. Once Raffaela was out of earshot, she walked to the breakfast table.

"You both should be ashamed of yourselves, behaving like this!" she said while trying to keep her voice from getting shrill.

Her mother raised her eyebrows. "I'm not the one who started it, dear."

Sabrina turned her face up toward the ceiling. "Why do I even bother?" Then she turned on her heels and headed back to the kitchen counter, when she saw Holly enter.

"Morning!" Holly greeted everybody cheerfully, then instantly joined Sabrina when their gazes met.

Holly put a hand on her shoulder and leaned in. "What's going on?"

Sabrina motioned to the breakfast table. "They keep sniping at each other. It's like I'm fourteen again, and they're in the middle of the divorce."

Holly rubbed Sabrina's shoulder in an attempt to comfort her. "Sorry, sweetheart. Just try and block it out."

Sabrina sniffed.

"What the hell?!" her father suddenly ground out.

Wondering what he and her mother were up to now, Sabrina whirled around, but her father wasn't glaring at his ex-wife. He'd jumped up and was staring at Sabrina, his finger pointing at the newspaper.

"What is this? A joke?" His stabbed his finger at a spot on the newspaper.

Sabrina shuddered internally. No! This couldn't be happening. This couldn't be the paper from that day . . . .

"What are you on about, George?" her mother asked, her voice sharp.

"This!" He shoved the newspaper in front of her, pointing to a spot.

Sabrina's legs carried her closer. And with every step, the knot in her stomach tightened as if it were a noose around her neck.

When she reached the table, her mother lifted her head from the paper and looked at her. Sabrina didn't have to look at what she'd been reading; she could see it in her mother's confused facial expression.

"Surely, that's a mistake," her mother said, looking at her with pleading eyes.

Sabrina felt Holly rush to her side and was glad to know she wasn't alone, though she had no idea how to explain the situation to her parents.

"It's all a lie," she managed to say, her voice dry as sandpaper. She pointed to the article. "One of Daniel's enemies is trying to cause trouble."

Her father shook his head. "Trouble? I'd say that's trouble!" His cheeks started to turn red.

"Then it's not true what they say here about you and Daniel, that you're his . . . uh . . . escort?" her mother asked, her voice sounding like she wanted to believe any explanation, as long as it meant that her daughter wasn't what the article accused her of.

Frantically, Sabrina shook her head. "No, Mom, it's all a lie. It's all fabricated."

Her mother closed her eyes and nodded to herself. "Good, then—"

"Fabricated? No newspaper prints a story like this without some sort of proof!" her father interrupted. "They must have a source for all this!"

"Their source lied. I'm not what they say I am!" Sabrina protested, leaning closer, hoping to convince her father of the truth.

"Then if it's a lie, why haven't you sued them yet?" He pointed to the date on the top right corner of the paper. "This was published five days ago."

"It's a misunderstanding. They got the wrong person. A lawsuit takes time. It's complicated." How could she tell her father that part of the evidence the paper had—Daniel's credit card statements—wouldn't help to discredit the reporter's source?

"Complicated? Goddamn it, Sabrina! It's in the paper! It's in black and white! If you're not suing immediately for defamation, everybody will believe it's true!" Her father's face turned even redder as if he were about to burst an artery. "Why would they publish something like this if there's not an ounce of truth to it?"

"But it's not true!" Helplessness spread over her. She knew how it looked to her parents, and the fact that she had no explanation she could give them, made things even worse. "Please, you have to trust me when I tell you that the story is false."

Her father shook his head. "How can I trust you when you can't tell me why they would say something like this about you? And why you're not doing anything about it." His mouth set into a grim line. "You leave me no choice but to believe what's in the paper."

Sabrina sniffed. "Please—"

But he cut her off. "How could you do this to me? How could you besmudge my good name like this?"

Her mother shot up from her chair. "Who are you gonna believe, your daughter or some slimy gossip columnist?"

"Selling her body like a common—"

"Don't say it!" her mother warned, her voice cold as ice.

Tears shot to Sabrina's eyes. "I'm not—" She pointed to the paper. "—that. Please, Dad, you have to believe me."

She felt Holly move next to her, putting her arm around Sabrina's waist to support her, while her mother did the same on the other side.

"It's all lies," Holly insisted.

"Stay out of this!" her father snapped. "You're probably not any better than her!"

Holly's gasp was drowned out by Raffaela's voice coming from the door. "What is going on here?"

Sabrina's father pointed at Sabrina. "She's a call girl! And your son is just another one of her clients!" He pointed to the newspaper that now lay on the table. "It's right there in the paper. Everybody knows! My name is being dragged through the mud!"

Her mother let go of Sabrina and leaned toward him, her chest heaving. "For fuck's sake, George! If anybody ever dragged your name through the mud, then it's you!"

"Shut it, Ilene! This is not about me! This is about your tramp of a daughter!"

"She's your daughter too, and she's not a tramp!"

"Believe what you want to believe! But I'm not going to be a part of this charade any longer!" He stormed out of the kitchen.

"Dad! Please! Don't leave!" Sabrina called after him, but he didn't even turn his head, as if he hadn't heard her.

A sob tore from her chest and a moment later she found herself pressed against Holly's chest and let her tears run freely. She barely heard the quiet words Raffaela and her mother exchanged.

Then the sound of footsteps came from the hallway and Daniel's voice drifted to her. "What happened?"

Holly released her from her hold, and Daniel pulled her into his arms. "Sabrina, baby, what's wrong?" He held her tightly, stroking her back, but she was unable to speak, her tears choking her.

"Her father saw the article in the *New York Times*," Raffaela explained. "Sabrina tried to explain to him that it's all a misunderstanding, but he wouldn't listen."

Daniel pressed kisses on top of her head. "I'm so sorry, baby. I'll fix this, I promise."

Sabrina lifted her head. In the periphery she saw Tim standing near the door, looking at her with pity in his eyes.

"Oh, Daniel, what are we gonna do?"

"I'll take care of it."

Just then, heavy footsteps came running down the stairs and a moment later, the front door was slammed. This couldn't be happening! But it was. When she heard the engine of a sports car rev up an instant later, she knew it: her father was leaving.

"He's not going to walk me down the aisle." She sobbed uncontrollably.

Daniel pressed her tighter to him. "I'll talk to him. I'll explain everything."

"But he's leaving!"

"Tim, take my car, follow him!" He tossed his keys to his friend. "Find out where he's going and keep me posted. I have to stay with Sabrina right now."

"It's no use," Sabrina murmured. Her father would fly home, thinking the worst of her, and he would refuse to speak to her.

Four days before her wedding, the cracks in her perfect world were starting to widen. What else would happen to bring her entire house of cards down?

20

Daniel brushed over Sabrina's hair as he rocked her in his arms. He'd brought her to their bedroom to grant Sabrina some peace and quiet. It was buzzing in the house now; the workers had arrived to build a platform in the garden, where the ceremony would take place, and others were busy finalizing the construction of the tent.

Tim had managed to catch up with Sabrina's father, who hadn't driven very far. He'd stopped in East Hampton, and according to Tim, he was still there, sitting in a coffee shop, brooding over a cup of coffee. Tim had not approached him. Later, once he'd calmed down a little, Daniel would have a word with him and convince him that the article was a lie, and that his daughter was a decent woman.

"How about I take you out for brunch? Just you and me. Nobody else," Daniel now asked Sabrina. "You need a little break from all this."

Sabrina lifted her head and sniffed. "What are we gonna do about my dad?"

Daniel softly stroked her cheek. "He'll come around. I'll take care of it. Promise. Now, you need a change of scenery."

He lifted her off his lap.

"I must look horrible." She wiped her face with her hands.

"You look beautiful as always," he said, though he didn't like to see the red puffiness around her eyes.

"Let me just freshen up a little."

"I'll wait for you downstairs."

When he reached the foot of the stairs, he leaned against the wall and stared at his shoes, contemplating his next actions.

"How is she?"

He looked up and stared at Holly, who'd approached without him noticing. "A little better. I'm taking her out for brunch at the country club, just the two of us."

"Good idea." Holly looked over her shoulder and leaned closer. "I've got news."

From above, he heard footsteps. Sabrina was walking down the stairs.

Holly glanced up, then whispered to him, "Tell you later," and hurried away.

When Sabrina reached him, her handbag slung over her shoulder and a cardigan draped over her arm, he greeted her with a smile. The last few days had taken their toll on her, and what they both needed was to spend time with each other on their own.

He took her hand. "I know a great place where we can relax a little."

Though she nodded and smiled, she'd clearly forced the smile for his sake. It broke his heart a little right there. Her father had accused her of terrible things, and he knew that it wouldn't be something she would be able to put behind her very easily. But Daniel would do everything in his power to make her father apologize to her and beg her to be allowed to walk her down the aisle on her wedding day.

In the car, Sabrina barely spoke, and he didn't press her. He knew her well enough that when she was hurt, she retreated into herself. She wasn't the kind of person to show everybody that she was hurt. She simply withdrew into her shell, just like she did now. Trying to force her to come back out when she wasn't ready to talk would be of no use. So he merely put his right hand over hers and held it while they were driving along the highway with the top of his convertible down.

When he pulled the car to a stop in front of the Maidstone Country Club and pulled into an empty parking spot, he let go of her hand.

"They serve a wonderful brunch here."

Sabrina gave him a grateful smile. "It's beautiful."

Daniel escorted her into the club house, through the elaborate entrance hall, and steered her toward the dining room, where a man wearing a beige summer suit stood at a podium, greeting the guests.

"Mr. Sinclair, so nice to see you," the man greeted him with a tight smile. It appeared the Maitre d' had read the article in the *New York Times*. He hadn't thought of how widely read the *New York Times* was among the residents of the Hamptons.

"Good morning, Eric," Daniel said evenly. "Two for brunch please. Maybe—"

"—somewhere quiet in the garden?" Eric suggested.

It appeared that the Maitre d' wanted to seat Daniel as far away as possible from the other respectable guests. Had Daniel not been with Sabrina, he would have taken exception to the man's presumption and insisted on being seated in the middle of the dining room, but in Sabrina's current vulnerable state, he wanted as little attention as possible. At least at the club where his entire family were members, nobody would dare make a scene. It was the reason he'd brought Sabrina here rather than taking her to one of the popular restaurants in Montauk or East Hampton, where they would possibly not receive such courtesy.

When Eric seated them in a quiet area in the garden, away from the main dining room, and immediately sent the waiter to them to take their drinks order, Daniel finally breathed a sigh of relief. He could feel Sabrina doing the same.

"Thank you. I just needed to get away from it all." She looked at him and smiled, but her eyes were clouded with a sadness that made his gut clench.

"I hate to see you like this." He took her hand and pressed a kiss onto its back. "Tell me what I can do."

She looked into the distance where several men were playing tennis. "I wish there were something you could do. But there isn't. It's all a mess."

"It will all work out in the end. Trust me."

"It won't change what my father thinks of me."

"It will, once they've retracted the story and issued an apology."

She whirled her head to him. "Even if they retract the story, because you're threatening to sue them, people will still think it's true."

"They won't if we can give the newspaper a story that will expose their previous story as a totally fabricated lie."

Sabrina dropped her lids. "It'll be too late. The wedding is in four days."

"Please, trust me—"

"Daniel," a male voice suddenly came from behind him.

He whirled his head around and saw Brian Caldwell stopping next to his and Sabrina's table. He was surprised to see his business associate here.

"When I called your house they told me I could find you here. So I figured, I'd talk to you in person."

Daniel stood up. "Brian, how are you? May I introduce my fiancée, Sabrina Parker?"

Brian nodded curtly, then his eyes darted back to Daniel. "Listen, I'm gonna make this short. My father wanted to send a letter to your lawyers and notify you, but I told him I'd rather tell you face to face. I think I owe you that much."

A knot formed in Daniel's gut. Whenever a business partner started the conversation like this, it never ended well. He glanced briefly at Sabrina and noticed that she was watching them intently.

"Can't this wait?"

Brian shook his head, regret evident in his eyes. "I'm really sorry. But you know that Caldwell's is a family company and has a certain reputation. My father has built the business from the ground up and done so without ever compromising his integrity. That's what we're built on. Our family values."

"What is your point?" Daniel interrupted.

Brian sighed. "My point is, we can't go through with the business deal. If we associate ourselves with you, it will . . . uh . . . taint our reputation."

"You want to toss a multi-million dollar deal out the window because your reputation might be *tainted* in the process?"

Brian chanced a look in Sabrina's direction as if his words needed any further explanation. "We can't afford a scandal like this. You must understand."

"Oh, I understand," Daniel responded coolly, but inside he was fuming.

Brian and his father were backing out of the business deal they'd been working out for the last couple of months, because they didn't want to be associated with a man whom they believed was marrying an escort.

He watched as Brian turned and left hastily, as if even a second longer in his and Sabrina's company would implicate him in the same scandal.

21

Sabrina looked up at Daniel, who was still standing. "I'm ruining your life."

He pulled the chair next to her back and sat down, leaning toward her. Her chest hurt, and she knew it wasn't a physical pain though it felt like one. It hurt because she realized she had to take action now, before everything got even worse. She had no choice but to save what could still be saved.

"No, you're not." He made a dismissive hand movement in the direction in which Brian Caldwell had left. "People pulling out of business deals happens all the time. It's nothing new."

She shook her head and let out a resigned sigh. "You're a terrible liar, Daniel. We both know why this deal fell apart. It's because of me. Because of what they think I am. It's never going to stop, is it?" She was certain of it. People in this town would always let her feel what they thought of her, just like Mrs. Teller and the woman from the lingerie store had. And now Brian Caldwell. And he wouldn't be the last.

Daniel's mouth set into a grim line. She knew then that she'd hit a nerve. "It will once they print the retraction."

"But they're not printing it, are they? We're four days away from the wedding, and everybody still thinks it's true. Your mother keeps getting more and more cancellations from guests. Daniel, this isn't affecting only me. It's affecting you, your business, your family."

And she didn't want to be responsible for destroying the lives of the people she loved.

"We'll get through this together."

Sabrina took a deep breath and prepared herself for what she had to do. The sadness that spread inside her felt like a cold hand that was trying to choke the life out of her. "The looks and whispers, the lies and accusations, they will destroy us. Today it's one business partner pulling out of a deal, tomorrow it's another. Don't you see that this will only get worse? Your whole livelihood is at stake. And your parents? Do you think they will really stand by and watch all this without secretly wishing I weren't there anymore?"

Daniel jerked back, his jaw dropping open, his chest lifting. "What are you saying?"

She looked at him with longing. She'd never loved a man like she loved him, but love wasn't enough for a life together. Not anymore. If she only had herself to think of, she would meet the challenge head-on and weather the storm, take the insults, the snide remarks, the shunning, and not flinch. But this wasn't about her alone anymore. She couldn't bring a child into this situation. She couldn't do that to their unborn child.

"My parents love you. They're standing by us." Daniel put his hands on her shoulders and peered into her eyes. "It doesn't matter what anyone else thinks. You and I know the truth, and we love each other. We don't need anything else."

Yes, they loved each other, and she didn't know how she could go on without feeling his love. But because she loved him, she had to make this decision, or one day he'd hate her for having ruined his life.

With a sad smile she shook her head. "It's not enough. Don't you understand? As long as this story is out there uncontested, nothing will ever be right."

"They will retract it."

"When?" she murmured, knowing that Daniel was stalling. By the look on his face he knew it too.

Daniel sighed. "I don't know. Soon."

"I'm sorry, Daniel. *Soon* isn't enough. I think we made a mistake."

"What kind of mistake?"

"We shouldn't get married." When the words were out, her heart clenched painfully, and she knew now what true pain felt like: as if somebody were slicing her heart into thin strips.

"Not get married?" Daniel stared at her in shock.

"This relationship was doomed from the start."

"Doomed?" he repeated. "Don't say that!"

"It started with a lie and spiraled downhill from there. It seems like no matter how hard we try, something or someone is always getting in our way." She rose, her legs so shaky she was wondering if she would collapse if she took a step.

Daniel grabbed her arm, getting up at the same time. "Don't do this!"

"Please let me go! Don't make this any harder than it already is," she demanded softly. "I can't marry you. This scandal will eventually destroy your life, your reputation, your business. And I could never live with myself knowing that I'm responsible for it. I can't carry that burden."

Because it would be hard enough to care for their child on her own. To raise it without it ever finding out what her mother had done. To love it so much that it would never know of the father's love she was depriving her child of.

"Sabrina, you're overreacting. Your father upset you. In a day or two you'll feel different. Please!" His gaze locked with hers. "Don't do this!"

"I'm sorry." Sabrina slid her engagement ring from her finger and held it out to him with shaking hands. The gold seemed to burn in her palm.

Daniel refused to take the ring. "We can work this out, Sabrina. We've done it before, and I know we can do it again."

She shook her head, her mind spinning and her eyes welling up with tears she desperately tried to suppress. "I love you, Daniel, but I can't stand by and watch your life get destroyed because of this. One day you'll know I was right. You'll thank me then."

With her last ounce of strength, she put the ring on the table and drew in a shaky breath. If she didn't get out of here right now, she would burst into tears, and Daniel would put his arms around her. And then, her resolve would crumble.

She turned on her heels and nearly collided with the waiter carrying a tray of drinks. She slid past him quickly, not wanting to give Daniel a chance to stop her. She couldn't allow it.

"Excuse me, sir, your drinks," she heard the waiter say, as she hurried away.

Keeping her head down so she wouldn't meet the eye of any of the club's guests, she rushed through the dining area, then entered the foyer.

She reached into her purse without stopping and felt for the spare key for Daniel's car. Clutching it tightly in her palm, she ran outside and unlocked the car. When she turned the key, the engine howled. She put it in gear and backed out of the parking spot, turned and drove down the long driveway leading away from the country club. Her movements seemed mechanical as if somebody else were steering her body.

Her vision became blurred, and she brought her hand to her eyes, wiping away her tears. She had to get away from here and start a new life where nobody knew her. Away from the scandal. Away from the lies. Away from Daniel.

Her baby would never have to listen to the lies about her. It would never have to hear them call her a whore.

22

Daniel looked after Sabrina in disbelief. This couldn't be happening!

"Sir, the drinks," the waiter repeated.

"We're not staying. Put the charge on my account." Daniel tried to squeeze between the waiter and a potted plant, when the waiter moved in the same direction. "Excuse me," Daniel ground out, watching as Sabrina disappeared inside the club building.

Finally the waiter moved out of his way, and he was able to pass and run after Sabrina. He didn't care who found his hasty departure curious.

The Maitre d' tossed him a displeased look, when Daniel charged past him and stormed into the lobby, then outside. He got there just in time to see Sabrina speed away in his sports car.

Daniel stomped his foot on the ground. "Fuck!"

He'd forgotten that she had a spare key to his car, and hadn't expected that she would leave him in the dust like this.

As he watched her disappear, a dark Mercedes with tinted windows pulled up and stopped in front of the entrance to the club house. The passenger door opened, and Linda Boyd stepped out.

Daniel inwardly groaned. Linda was the last person he wanted to see right now. He tried to turn away to avoid her, but it was too late. She'd obviously spotted him from afar and was already making a beeline for him.

"Hi Daniel, I thought that was your car driving past us."

There was no use denying it. Linda knew his car as well as anybody else who knew him. And with the top being down, she would also have had no trouble seeing that Sabrina was driving it.

Tensing, he greeted her, "Linda."

She smiled at him, either oblivious to the fact that he wasn't in the mood to talk, or blatantly ignoring it. "Sabrina just dropped you off here? If we'd known that you needed to get to the club, we would have given you a ride." She motioned to the black Mercedes which was just pulling into a parking spot.

"Thanks, but it was no bother." Under no circumstances would he let on that Sabrina had just broken off their engagement.

Oh God! He couldn't believe it. Everything had gone so fast. Had she really called off the wedding?

"Mr. Sinclair!" he heard a voice call out for him from inside the foyer.

Daniel whipped his head around and watched as the waiter hurried toward him, reaching out his hand. Something glittered in the midday sunlight.

Before his brain could fully comprehend what was going on, the waiter pressed Sabrina's engagement ring into Daniel's palm, driving home reality once more. Sabrina had left him.

"Your fiancée left her ring on the table, sir," the waiter said politely, before turning back to the club house's entrance.

Daniel cringed.

"Oh dear," Linda said. While her voice sounded full of regret and pity, her facial expression said otherwise. When her hand touched his forearm, he almost jolted. "Is it because of Paul Gilbert? I'm so sorry, if I'd known it would come to this, I would have told you about them. I just didn't think there was anything to it. It looked so innocent."

Daniel's eyes narrowed. "What are you talking about?"

"Well, about Sabrina and Paul meeting in East Hampton the other day. You know. They were embracing in public. I figured there's nothing to it. It wasn't like they were trying to hide it."

Daniel forced himself to take a couple of deep breaths. He recognized when somebody was trying to manipulate him. And Linda was clearly manipulating him. But even in the state he was in, it didn't work, though he wanted to find a different reason why Sabrina had left him—a reason he could do something about. A reason he could beat to a pulp and obliterate. But no such reason existed. He knew it in his gut.

"Paul and Sabrina have nothing going on. So stay out of this, Linda!" he ground out firmly. Though he knew that Paul enjoyed flirting, he trusted Sabrina fully. But why had neither of them mentioned the meeting? During the bachelor party Paul had even innocently asked how Sabrina was doing, as if he hadn't seen her in ages.

"Your friend Audrey has caused enough trouble. So you'll do well not pissing me off any further."

He turned away from her, intent on hailing the cab parked at the taxi stand across the driveway, but two people blocked his way: Kevin had gotten out of the Mercedes and walked up to them, Audrey next to him.

He hadn't anticipated seeing her. His heartbeat raced. For a long moment neither of them said a word.

Then Audrey purred, "Well, hello." Her eyes dropped to the ring in his hand, and a smile started curving her lips upwards. "I think my work is done." She let out a laugh.

Daniel took a step closer to her, going toe-to-toe. "If you think your lies are going to drive Sabrina and me apart, you're wrong. I will prove that the article is a lie!"

Audrey shrugged. "Too late! By the looks of it, it worked. Seems like there won't be a wedding after all. What a shame. Your parents will be so disappointed. And they will be the laughingstock of the entire community."

She made an attempt to step past him, but he grabbed her upper arm. "Watch out, Audrey. I will take you down!"

He let go of her and hurried past her, jumping into the taxi.

"Drive!" he instructed the driver and pulled his cell phone from his pocket.

He had to put his mind to rest by clarifying one thing first before going home to stop Sabrina from packing and returning to New York. The call was connected almost immediately.

"Hey Daniel, forgot something?" Zach asked.

"Is Paul still with you?"

"No, he and Jay left a half hour ago to have lunch at Frank's Crab Shack."

"Thanks." He disconnected the call without any further explanation. "Drive me to Frank's Crab Shack, please," he instructed the cab driver instead.

The drive from the Maidstone Country Club to the Crab Shack took only minutes, but to Daniel they felt like hours.

When the cab finally came to a stop, Daniel paid the driver and got out. He entered the restaurant, perused the people sitting at the tables inside, and walked through to the terrace that faced the beach.

He saw Paul and Jay sitting at a table at the end, plates with fresh crab legs in front of them. He approached without them noticing him, the two seemingly deep in conversation.

When Daniel reached the table, he tapped on Paul's shoulder, making him snap his head toward him.

"Hey, Daniel! Wanna join us? There's more than enough food!" Paul motioned to the mountain of crab in the middle of the table.

Daniel ignored the question. "Why were you and Sabrina meeting in town the other day?" His heart hammered in his chest.

Paul almost visibly choked on the crab in his mouth. He reached for his beer and took a deep gulp, all the while his eyes stared at Daniel in utter surprise.

"We ran into each other," Paul finally answered.

"Are you saying it was a coincidence?" Daniel asked.

"Of course! Why wouldn't it?" Paul exchanged a quick glance with Jay, who'd set down his crab leg and watched the exchange with interest, remaining silent.

"You were seen embracing her." Daniel watched as Paul's facial expression changed to one of defensiveness.

"Hey! Hold on here! That was entirely innocent."

"Then why did neither of you mention it to me? Why do I have to find out from Linda Boyd?"

Paul shook his head. "That gossip mongering bitch! There was nothing to it, Daniel. I might have flirted with Sabrina in the past. *Before* you got engaged. But I draw the line when things get serious between a couple. It's true, I was hugging Sabrina, but I was only comforting her."

Daniel's forehead furrowed. "Comforting?"

"Didn't she tell you how people in the village were treating her? She was thrown out of Lisette's lingerie store. The owner was downright nasty to her. Sabrina was in tears. All I did was try and get her out of there in one piece. And of course Linda misconstrues it to mean something else. You should know that she only spews venom!"

Daniel raked a hand through his hair, relieved on one hand, concerned on the other. He should have anticipated that people in the village wouldn't be kind after they'd read the article. But that somebody had actually thrown Sabrina out of a store, seemed to go too far. "Why didn't Sabrina tell me?"

"She probably didn't want you to go down there and make a fuss."

Paul was right. Daniel would have gone to the shop and given the owner a piece of his mind. "Sorry, man."

"No harm done. Now that everything's fine again, wanna join us for a beer and some crab legs?"

Daniel shook his head. "Nothing is fine."

Both his friends stared at him expectantly.

"Sabrina left me. She called off the wedding." Daniel dropped onto the bench next to Paul and put his head in his hands.

"Why?" Jay asked.

"She doesn't want to ruin my life, and as long as the article is out there and hasn't been retracted and exposed as a lie, she thinks she's destroying my life and my business."

"How so?" Paul wanted to know.

"Brian Caldwell came to see me to let me know that he and his father are pulling out of the deal because of the scandal. They don't want to be associated with me anymore."

"And Sabrina knows about it?" Jay asked.

"She was there when it happened." Daniel rested his chin on his hand. How could he ever live without Sabrina? She was his life, his everything.

Jay rubbed the back of his neck. "Listen, I know I shouldn't say this, but under the circumstances . . . if you're not getting married, what are you guys gonna do about the baby?"

Daniel's head whipped back up. "What baby?"

Jay pulled back. "Oops."

"Jay, out with it!"

"Well, I promised I wasn't gonna tell you, but . . . " He sighed. "Maybe I'm wrong and the test was negative. But I saw her at the OBGYN's office with her friend Holly, and once a woman goes to see an OBGYN, chances are she wants to confirm a pregnancy, because her home pregnancy test was positive."

Sabrina could be pregnant? Was it possible?

Daniel jumped up from the table. He had to stop Sabrina from doing anything foolish.

23

When the taxi dropped him off in front of his parents' home, Daniel knew immediately that Sabrina wasn't here: his car wasn't parked in the driveway. Had she gone for a drive somewhere to cool off? Or worse, had she already been here, packed her things and left?

He tossed the taxi driver way too much money and jumped out of the cab, then ran to the entrance door, jammed his key in the lock and unlocked it.

Inside the foyer, he called, "Sabrina!" But in his gut, he knew she was gone. She'd taken off. He charged upstairs, but found the bedroom they'd shared empty. However, Sabrina's things were still strewn about.

He pulled out his cell and dialed her number, pacing in the room while it rang. After the fourth ring it went to her voicemail. He'd expected that she wouldn't pick up.

"Please, Sabrina, come back. We need to talk," he said, before disconnecting the call.

Daniel made his way downstairs again, this time heading for the kitchen, from where he heard voices. When he entered, he was relieved to see that only Holly and his mother were in the room. He wouldn't have been able to face Sabrina's mother right now.

"Have you seen Sabrina?" he asked without a greeting.

His mother turned halfway while she continued to mix dough in a large bowl. "I thought you took her out for brunch."

He raked a shaky hand through his hair. "I did. But she left."

"Oh, I'm sure she'll be back soon then," his mother said lightly and walked to the larder to pull out a bag of flour. "I think I got my measurements all mixed up today," she added with a sideways glance to Holly.

"That's just it: I don't think she'll come back."

Holly turned to him first, her eyes widening. Then his mother turned too and gave him her full attention.

"What do you mean, she's not coming back?" Holly asked, drawing out the words.

Daniel closed his eyes for a moment. "She gave me back her engagement ring." He drew in a ragged breath. "She called off the wedding."

The moment he said it, he knew it was true. Sabrina wasn't a woman to make empty threats in order to get attention.

Both Holly and his mother gasped.

"Oh my god! No!" His mother shook her head as if she could make the news go away like that. "That can't be. What happened? What did you do?"

"But she loves you," Holly professed.

"That's just it. She left me because she loves me. She doesn't want to ruin my life because of this scandal."

"Is this because of her father running out like that?" His mother motioned to the breakfast table as if he were still sitting there.

"Partially. I think it's everything: the way people in the village have been treating her, her father calling her terrible things, and then when we were at the country club . . . " He hesitated.

"What happened?" Holly pressed.

"One of my business associates stopped by to tell me that he's pulling out of a business deal because of what the *New York Times* printed. I think it was the last straw for her."

"You can't let her just leave!" his mother said, wiping her hands on her apron. "You have to get her back. Didn't you tell her that none of this matters? You can't possibly put your business before her."

"Of course not!" he ground out, for the first time glaring at his mother. "I told her I don't care about the business deal. But she wouldn't listen. She's convinced that she'll ruin my life if she marries me."

"Then you have to convince her otherwise!" his mother demanded.

He nodded grimly. Then he looked at Holly. "There's one thing I have to know. And you're the only one who can tell me, Holly."

Holly lifted her eyebrows.

"Is Sabrina pregnant?"

For a second not a sound could be heard in the kitchen. His mother was holding her breath, and Holly seemed to contemplate her answer.

"Holly!" he urged her. "Jay saw you and Sabrina at the OBGYN's office the other day."

Holly blinked. "The doctor confirmed it. She's seven weeks pregnant."

His heart started to hammer and seemed to overshadow even his mother's loud gasp. "Does she want my baby?"

"What kind of question is that? Of course she wants your baby!"

"Why didn't she tell me then?"

"She wanted to tell you on your wedding night."

Though the way things stood now, there wouldn't be a wedding night. "I have to find her. Now."

"Wait!" Holly stopped him.

Daniel stared at her, wondering what else there was to say.

"You won't be able to change her mind. Nothing has changed. The situation is still the same: the scandal is causing your business to suffer. Sabrina won't simply take your word for it that you don't care about that. You've already tried that. You have to get the story retracted before Sabrina will talk to you."

"Damn it, Holly, we already tried that. Neither talking to the newspaper reporter nor threatening Audrey has helped. I called my attorney and he's already preparing everything to sue the newspaper, but a lawsuit is a drawn-out process. They won't retract the story in the next few days. I've tried everything."

"Not everything," Holly said. "I wanted to tell you before you left for brunch. I have news."

"What news?"

"I'll show you on my computer." She motioned him to follow her out of the kitchen.

"What are you doing?" his mother called after them.

Holly turned briefly. "Trust us, we'll get Sabrina back, but the fewer people know about this the better."

Daniel followed her up to her room, his pulse racing all the while. He could only hope that whatever Holly had wasn't just news, but *good* news.

Holly walked to her computer and booted it up. "Remember that we talked about trying to convince the paper that it was all a case of mistaken identity?"

"Yes, but we already ruled it out because it would expose you."

"Oh, I'm not talking about myself." She navigated to a website, then clicked on a link and scrolled farther down until a picture appeared on the screen.

A photo of Sabrina with a slightly different hairstyle greeted him. It had to have been taken before he'd met her, since her hair was longer and wavier in the picture.

He raised an eyebrow. "How is an old photo of Sabrina good news? And what is it doing on a website?"

Holly grinned. "Guess she just passed the test."

"What test?" Daniel's forehead furrowed.

"If you can't tell that this isn't Sabrina, then nobody else can either."

He pointed to the picture, looking at it more closely now. "This is not Sabrina?"

"No."

Daniel blew out a breath. He suddenly knew exactly what Holly was trying to do. "Oh my god!" He hugged her, lifting her off her feet and making a full circle before he set her down again.

"Okay, okay. We're not out of the woods yet. We've got work to do. I've found out that she lives in Colorado. There's a phone number and an email address."

"How can I help?" he asked eagerly.

"We need to hire her to come to New York, go to the newspaper office and tell them she's the escort the columnist's source is referring to. The columnist will look at her, then at Sabrina's picture and realize she's practically her twin. We'll have to pay her of course."

"I don't care what it costs."

"Do you know anybody who's got a jet to fly her from Colorado to New York? I'm afraid if we book her on a commercial airline, we'll be losing time."

Daniel nodded instantly. "I'll talk to Zach. His company has a couple of jets. Maybe one of them is out west. If not, he'll know somebody else whom we can borrow a plane from."

Holly made a note on a small notepad next to her computer. "Good." She tapped with her pen on the paper, clearly contemplating something. "That leaves us with only one problem."

"What problem? It looks clear to me." He pointed to the screen where the picture of the woman who looked like Sabrina still stared at him. "This woman will show the reporter her ID and prove that she's not Sabrina. The reporter will realize that it was a case of mistaken identity and issue an apology."

"Yes, but there's still one loose end: your credit card statement. Audrey gave a copy of your credit card statement to the reporter. It shows the charge to the escort agency. How will you explain that?"

Daniel rubbed the back of his neck. He hadn't thought about that, too ecstatic that Holly had found a woman who looked like the spitting image of Sabrina. "Crap!"

"Yes. I've been thinking about it ever since I found this photo. But I can't figure out how we can discredit the credit card statement. If we don't, then the reporter will think you hired an escort who looked like Sabrina. And I don't think she'll buy the whole story as long as there's a shred of evidence that you did hire an escort. If only that copy of the credit card statement didn't exist."

Yes, if only Frances hadn't given Audrey access to his confidential financial records! For that indiscretion Frances had deserved being fired. And she'd never get a decent reference out of him.

"That's it!" He'd just figured it out.

"What?" Holly stared at him with wide eyes.

"The credit card statement. Audrey only got a copy of it. If we can prove that the copy is a fake and that Audrey added in the charge to an escort agency to make it look like I hired Sabrina as an escort, then her whole story falls apart."

"True. But how are you gonna do that? If I may remind you: the charge is real. My agency did charge your credit card. Besides, if you suddenly produce a different copy, they'll think your copy is doctored, not hers."

For the first time since Sabrina had broken off their engagement, Daniel grinned. "I'm not gonna be the one who comes forward with a new copy. Frances is going to do that."

"Your assistant? I thought you fired her."

"And that's exactly why she'll do it: she needs a reference from me more than she needs anything else."

Holly chuckled. "You're positively evil." She winked at him. "I like it." Then she paused. "And how are you gonna make this copy look more real than the one Audrey gave to the reporter?"

"I'm gonna have Frances hand over the original."

"But the original contains the credit card charge."

Daniel put a hand on Holly's shoulder. "Did I ever tell you the story of how, when back in college, Wade would have nearly flunked out of statistics?"

Holly looked at him like he'd lost his mind. "Huh?"

"Well, let's just say his skills in graphic arts and Photoshop more than make up for it. In fact, it's a little hobby of his."

Holly's jaw dropped. "Are you telling me Wade is going to forge your credit card statement?"

Daniel smiled. "Let's get to work. You contact the girl. I'll talk to Zach, Wade, and Frances." He looked at his watch. "We're not gonna make the deadline for tomorrow's edition of the *New York Times*, but if we can fly this woman out to New York by tonight and Wade can get the credit card statement to Frances by courier first thing in the morning, the article will be retracted the day after."

And then he'd get Sabrina back.

24

Everything had happened like clockwork: Holly had convinced Sabrina's Doppelganger to come to New York and tell Claire Heart that *she* was the real escort, not Sabrina. The money Daniel had promised her had sealed the deal. Zach had been able to organize a private jet from a friend in Las Vegas who'd picked up Sabrina's Doppelganger in Denver and flown her to New York LaGuardia airport. Then a limousine hired by Zach's company had chauffeured her to the newspaper's offices.

Wade had worked all afternoon and night on reproducing the credit card statement which Daniel had been able to access online. In the early hours of the morning, Wade had presented Daniel with two sheets of paper that looked so real Daniel couldn't tell that they were forged. Instead of hiring a courier, Wade had taken it upon himself to drive the document to Frances' apartment in Brooklyn and delivered it into her hands.

In the meantime, Daniel had called Harvey, the doorman of his condo building and found out that Sabrina had indeed returned to New York. He'd asked him to let him know if he thought she was leaving. Under a pretext, Harvey had gone up to the apartment and noticed that Sabrina was packing boxes. But even Daniel knew that she wouldn't be able to hire movers in a day or two.

Nevertheless, he was antsy by the time the second evening without Sabrina rolled around. He was pacing on the back porch, staring at the tent that was ready for the wedding, when his cell phone rang.

"Yes?"

"Mr. Sinclair, this is Claire Heart."

He silently pumped his fist in the air, but kept the excitement out of his voice. He couldn't let the reporter know that he knew what had been happening in her office today.

"Yes, Miss Heart? What other untruths are you planning on publishing about me and my fiancée next?"

"Uhm, Mr. Sinclair. I'm . . . I'm really sorry. I was trying to reach you earlier, but couldn't get through. There have been some developments. I'm not going to bore you with the details. But we've established that there's been a case of mistaken identity. We are very sorry for the grief we've caused you and your fiancée. In tomorrow's print edition you'll find a retraction of the article and an apology by the paper and myself, of course. And the online edition will go live with the story just after midnight."

"Well . . ."

"It has all been a terrible mistake. But as you can probably appreciate, sometimes the evidence that is presented to us looks very convincing."

"I understand, Miss Heart. Thank you for calling."

He disconnected the call and jumped into the air. "Yes!"

It had worked. Claire Heart and her editor and legal department had swallowed the story he and Holly had fabricated hook, line, and sinker.

Tomorrow, all of New York and the Hamptons would find out that Sabrina wasn't a call girl. Everything would go back to normal. But he couldn't wait till tomorrow. Hadn't the reporter said that the online edition would post the story shortly past midnight?

So what was he still doing here in Montauk? He should be on his way to his condo in Manhattan. Daniel glanced at his watch. If he left now, he'd arrive there just after midnight.

Minutes later, he was sitting in his father's car, speeding into the night, heading for New York.

***

Even though she was tired from packing, Sabrina couldn't sleep, so she didn't even try. Instead, she sat in the living room. Only a small lamp burned in one corner. Beyond the floor-to-ceiling windows, Manhattan sparkled like a thousand raindrops cascading over a mirror. It wasn't raining though; it was Sabrina's tears causing the skyline of Manhattan to appear blurred.

"It's for the best," she murmured to herself. "It's for you." She laid her hand over her stomach. She had to remain strong for her child. She didn't want it to be born into a community that shunned her parents. She'd rather disappear to somewhere where nobody knew her and raise the child on her own.

A sob tore from her chest. If only she were stronger and wouldn't miss Daniel so much. Another sob followed. More of them ripped from her chest and just wouldn't stop. She reached for a tissue and blew her nose.

"Don't cry."

Sabrina shrieked and whirled around, jumping up instantly. She hadn't heard the apartment door over her sobs.

Even in the relative dark of the room, she recognized him immediately. "Daniel," she managed to say.

Then he reached her and pulled her against his chest. She wanted to protest, but she was too weak.

"I'm here now," he murmured into her hair.

"It won't change anything." She pushed against him and eased away. He let it happen, and she was disappointed that he did.

His hands moved and suddenly another light source illuminated his face as he stared down at an iPad. He handed it to her. "Read this."

"What is this?"

"Just read it," he demanded. "Please."

Compelled by the tenderness in his eyes, she looked down at the screen. The first thing she saw was a photo of herself, though on closer inspection she knew it couldn't be she: the hair style was completely wrong, and the top the woman wore didn't belong to Sabrina either.

Her eyes dropped to the line below the picture. *Ms. Sharon Helmer* it said.

Then she read the headline: *Correction.*

Below it only a few lines were written.

On the 18th of this month, this paper published a story about Mr. Daniel Sinclair and Miss Sabrina Palmer. The information presented to the Times as the basis of this story has proven to be false. In fact, a Miss Sharon Helmer, pictured, has been mistaken for Miss Palmer. Miss Palmer is in no way connected to any escort service and there is no evidence that Mr. Sinclair, her fiancé, has ever used the services of an escort agency. We would like to extend our deepest apologies and sincerest regrets to Mr. Daniel Sinclair and Miss Sabrina Palmer and their families.

Sabrina lifted her head.

"You did it," she whispered. "You got them to retract the story. How?"

"I had some help," he said with a smile.

"But . . . this other woman. Who is she?"

"A model and escort. Holly found her and—"

Sabrina threw herself into his arms, cutting off his next words. "Thank you!"

She felt his warm lips on hers, lips she'd missed and craved for the last two days. His arms wrapped around her, holding her so tightly to him that she felt physically how much he'd missed her too.

His mouth devoured hers, his tongue stroking forcefully against hers, delving deep, reacquainting himself with her, while she was doing the same. It had been too long to be away from him. Right at that moment she realized that she would have never been able to leave him for good.

"God, I missed you!" he murmured when he severed the kiss. "Please don't ever leave me again."

"Never again, I promise."

"I'll hold you to your promise."

She reached for him, pulling his face back to her. "I want you."

"You've got me, baby, body and soul."

He tugged on her T-shirt and pulled it over her head, making her shiver despite the warmth in the apartment. His hands swept over her naked breasts, caressing them tenderly. She felt his touch more intensely now. The pregnancy had made her breasts more sensitive.

The pregnancy. Her heart stopped. She hadn't told him about it yet, but she didn't think she could keep it a secret until their wedding night. He needed to know, and she needed to tell him.

"Daniel," she whispered just as he dipped his head to one breast and sucked her hardened nipple into his mouth, pulling on it gently, while licking over it with the full breadth of his tongue. The texture of it rubbing over her receptive flesh made her shudder with pleasure.

"Yes?" he murmured against her flesh.

"There's something you need to . . . "

" . . . do?" he asked. "Anything you want, baby. You just tell me what you need."

"No, something you need to know," she tried again and took his head between both hands, lifting it off her breast and forcing him to look at her.

The passion that clouded his eyes made her womb clench in anticipation.

"I'm pregnant." She let out a breath. "I'm having your baby."

Warmth and adoration now radiated from his eyes. "I know, baby."

Surprised, her mouth dropped open. "You know?"

He nodded, his hand now sliding gently down her torso until it came to rest on her belly. He stroked over it in slow movements. "I should have noticed earlier. When I touch you now, I can feel the changes in your body. Your breasts are fuller and so much more responsive when I touch them. And when I look into your face, I can see the glow. You're radiant, Sabrina. I should have seen it. I should have known. It's no surprise that you took everything so hard. You had such a burden to carry, so much stress to deal with. I should have realized earlier that your hormones were making everything more difficult for you. Had I known . . ."

She put a finger over his lips, stopping him. "I wanted to find the perfect moment to tell you, but when everything took a turn for the worse, I couldn't. I didn't want you to feel obligated and marry me just because of the baby. Because I know you would have never let me go had you known."

Daniel shook his head and laughed softly. "Sabrina, let's be clear about one thing: I'll never let you go, pregnant or not. We belong together. Without you, I'm only half a man."

She pushed back the tear that threatened to run down her cheek at his loving words. "How did you find out? Holly?"

"After Jay let it slip that he saw you and Holly at the OBGYN office, I confronted her. She really had no choice but to tell me at that point. So don't be mad at her."

"I'm not." She kissed him softly.

"Good," he agreed. "Now, where were we?" He ran his eyes over her naked torso. "Oh, yes, I believe I was about to undress you completely and make love to you."

She reached for the top button of his polo shirt and opened it. "Then what are you doing standing there fully dressed?"

He stepped out of her arms and pulled his shirt over his head, tossing it to the ground. His shoes, pants, and boxer briefs followed.

Then he tugged on the string that tied her sweatpants at her waist and loosened the knot. The material dropped to the floor with a soft whoosh, leaving her standing in only a G-string.

Daniel hooked his thumbs under the fabric and pushed it down, helping her out of the flimsy garment. A moment later, he swept her up in his arms and brought her down to lie on the sofa, his body braced over hers.

"Baby, if anything hurts, you'll let me know, won't you?"

Her forehead furrowed. "Why would anything hurt?"

He slid his palm over her stomach. "I don't want to hurt the baby."

She chuckled and pulled him down to her. "I've read that a pregnant woman can have sex well into the final weeks of her pregnancy without hurting the baby in the slightest." Then her hand reached for his cock and wrapped around it. He was as hard as an iron rod, and it was exactly what she needed from him right now. She needed to feel him inside her, showing her how much he desired her. How much he loved her. "Take me."

"If you put it that way," he murmured and gripped her left thigh, urging her to open up to him.

Without breaking eye contact, Sabrina guided his cock to her sex, then released her grip on him. An instant later, he thrust forward and sliced into her in one continuous stroke until he was seated balls-deep.

She pressed her head into the pillow, her back arching off the sofa cushions as she received him. "Oh God!"

"Too hard?" he asked immediately and pulled back.

But before he could withdraw completely, she'd already slung her legs around him and crossed her ankles below his butt, imprisoning him. "You're not going anywhere."

Daniel shook his head, his eyes devouring her. "I don't deserve you." Despite his words, he plunged back into her. "But I'm not giving you up."

"You'd better not." She pulled his head to her and pressed her lips onto his mouth, kissing him with all the pent-up passion and love she felt for him. At the same time she poured all her hopes for a happy future into the kiss.

As they lay on the couch making love, the lights from the city reflected on their glistening bodies, moving as their bodies moved. In the semi-darkness of their living room, Sabrina felt renewed by the knowledge that Daniel would always come back for her, would never give up on her. And with his body he showed her that he desired only her, that his heart beat only for her. She felt it. With every thrust of his cock, she felt his heartbeat reverberate in her womb. With every kiss, she felt warmth spread in her heart.

"I love you," she whispered between panted breaths and strangled moans.

They were mere echoes of Daniel's sounds of pleasure as he took her more passionately and yet more tenderly than ever before. There was something reverent about the way he loved her tonight. As if he worshipped her.

Her entire body began to hum and vibrate under his ministrations, and she knew she couldn't hold her climax back any longer.

"Now," she urged. "Now, Daniel!"

He gazed into her eyes, and she could see it so clearly there: the love that needed no words. Then his eyes shut and he threw his head back. His jaw clenched and the cords in his neck tightened when he drew back and delivered another thrust.

With a moan, she let herself go and felt the waves of her orgasm wash over her at the same time as she felt the warmth of his semen flood her. His thrusts slowed as they rode out their climax together.

When Daniel finally stilled, he kissed her softly, then pushed a strand of her damp hair away from her cheek. He looked down at her as if he wanted to say something, but there was nothing that needed to be said. She could see it in his eyes.

He was happy to have her back. As was she.

25

Daniel held her hand as they walked to the back of the house where the tent was ready. Flowers were being brought in, and everything looked like a dream. But Sabrina knew it wasn't a dream. It was reality. A reality that nearly hadn't happened.

She squeezed Daniel's hand, causing him to look away from the goings-on in his parents' garden and gazing at her instead. His eyes shone with love when he murmured, "What?"

"Thank you for not giving up."

He reached up to her face and brushed his knuckles over her cheek. "I would never give up on you or on us. We belong together. And we've created something together. Something beautiful." He dropped his gaze to her stomach as if he could already see a bump forming there, though Sabrina knew she wouldn't show for another two months at least. "No matter what happens in the future, I'll never give up as long as there's any love left between us. It's worth fighting for it."

"You're not concerned that we're having a baby so early in our lives together?"

"No, though it's going to be hard to share you with somebody else who wants your love." Then he chuckled. "Good thing is that we'll have a very dedicated babysitter." He motioned toward the tent where his mother was giving the florist and her helpers instructions on where to place the flower arrangements.

Sabrina laughed. Her mother-in-law would be a wonderful grandmother. "I fear that once we hand our child over to her for a day, she won't want to give it back."

"That's a definite risk," Daniel admitted.

"Daniel?" his father's voice suddenly came from the house as he stepped out into the garden. When he spotted them, he added, "Ah, here you are. The Millers just called and said they're coming to the wedding, and they're very sorry about the mix-up with the calendars. They said they can make it after all." He rolled his eyes.

Daniel shook his head. "Mix-up? It appears the Millers just read the *New York Times* and decided that it's safe again to be associated with us."

His father smiled. "It appears so. So let's be gracious and welcome them. I've added them back onto the guest list."

Sabrina pointed toward Raffaela. "James, you might want to let your wife know. I have the feeling she'll want to rearrange the seating plan again."

James sighed. "Oh dear."

Sabrina stroked over his shoulder. "Well at least they're not invited to the rehearsal dinner tonight. If she had to change the arrangements for tonight, she would really be stressing out. At least there's still time to make changes for tomorrow."

Her future father-in-law made a dramatic grimace. "I'm assuming neither of you wants to do the honors?"

Both Daniel and Sabrina shook their heads in unison.

"You can do it, Dad," Daniel encouraged him as he marched toward his wife.

"Do you think we'll be like that when we're an old married couple?" Sabrina asked.

"You mean still in love? Still playful?" He pressed a soft kiss on her lips. "Yes, all of that. I promise you."

Before she could lean into him and kiss him back, footsteps from behind her made her turn her head.

Sabrina's breath caught in her chest. "Mrs. Vogel?"

The female partner of Yellin, Vogel, and Winslow, the firm who'd fired her only days earlier, stepped onto the porch. "I'm sorry, Miss Parker," she said hesitantly and pointed back toward the house. "The front door was open, and there was nobody in the house. I'm sorry to intrude." She motioned to the tent. "You're busy. So I won't keep you long."

Sabrina swallowed and instinctively reached for Daniel's hand.

"Mr. Sinclair." Mrs. Vogel nodded at Daniel. "I've come to apologize to both of you. On behalf of the entire firm, I'm terribly sorry for the manner in which we treated you. It was inexcusable. We should have known that it couldn't be true. We should have trusted in you and your integrity. I could give you a hundred excuses why we terminated your employment. You know, reputation, image and such. But what it boils down to was that we made an error in judgment. And for that we're truly sorry."

Sabrina nodded numbly, surprised at the thoughtful apology. "Thank you, Mrs. Vogel. It means a lot to me."

"That's not all. I know you might not trust us anymore, Miss Parker, but we do value your work at the firm. You're an excellent attorney, and we would hate it if we'd lost you for good. I'm here to offer you your job back. That is if you still want it."

Sabrina could barely believe her ears. "You're offering me my job back?"

With a smile, Mrs. Vogel nodded. "Take your time to make a decision. But we would love it if you returned to Yellin, Vogel, and Winslow after your honeymoon."

Sabrina exchanged a long look with Daniel, who smiled at her encouragingly. Then she looked back at Mrs. Vogel and stretched her hand out to her. "I'd love to."

Mrs. Vogel let out a relieved breath, shaking Sabrina's hand. "Thank you. And congratulations on your upcoming wedding."

Moments later Mrs. Vogel was gone.

"I can't believe it!" she said and threw herself into Daniel's arms.

He turned her in a circle as if she were a horse on a carousel.

"Congratulations, baby!" He laughed. "See, everything is fine now."

"Almost everything." She smiled wistfully. The wedding was back on. The guests were coming. She had her job back. But there was still one thing that wasn't right.

"I wish my father would come back and walk me down the aisle tomorrow."

Then everything would be perfect again.

26

"And you're sure he's still there?" Daniel asked Tim as they both got out of the car in front of the Mill House Inn in East Hampton.

Tim nodded. "I sweet-talked the girl who works the front desk. She would have called me if he'd checked out."

Daniel couldn't suppress a smirk. "A girl, really?"

"Hey, she totally thinks I'm straight." Tim shrugged. "Not my fault that her *gaydar* isn't working. Anyway, she hasn't called me. Looks like he's reluctant to leave after all. Maybe he just needs a gentle push in the right direction."

"I hope you're right. Do you know what room he's in?"

"Twenty-two. Up the stairs, turn right, then an immediate left." Tim's cell phone suddenly rang. He pulled it from his pocket and looked at the display. "It's the PI."

"Take it." Daniel watched as Tim answered the phone. They'd managed to get the story retracted without the PI's help, but it wouldn't hurt to find out what the private investigator had found out about Audrey.

"Yeah? This is Tim."

Lots of hmms, uh huhs, and ohs came over Tim's lips while he listened to the PI on the other end of the line. Then he finally said, "Email me the file. Thanks, man."

He hung up, a crooked grin on his face.

"He found something?" Daniel asked, curious now.

Tim chuckled. "Oh, you're so not gonna believe whom our little tramp Audrey slept with when she was sixteen."

"Whom?"

Tim shook his head. "Tell you afterward." He motioned to the entrance door of the B&B. "Now, go and give him a piece of your mind. I'll wait here and make a few calls."

Daniel didn't press Tim for an explanation, opened the door to the beautiful building and stepped into the foyer with the dark wooden floors and the white walls which were hung with pictures of old ships and other maritime motifs. He glanced to the little reception area. A sign stood on the counter next to a little bell: *Ring me for service!*

Just as well that nobody was manning the reception. He much preferred going upstairs without being seen. Following Tim's instructions, he found the room in question immediately. He knocked and waited.

There was a sound coming from the inside, then the door was opened.

Sabrina's father wore a pair of pants and a wife-beater shirt. He looked unshaven and unkempt. Daniel inhaled. And he'd been drinking, he added to his quick assessment.

"What do you want?" George Palmer asked.

"I want to talk to you."

By way of reply, George opened the door wider and stepped aside. Daniel entered, closing the door behind him, and looked around. The TV was on mute. The *New York Times* lay on the sofa in front of it, and a bottle of Jim Beam stood on the side table, a half empty glass next to it.

Daniel took a closer look at the newspaper and was able to read the date: it was today's edition.

"You read it?" he asked George without turning his head to him.

George walked around and slumped down on the couch. "Yeah."

"So you know it was all a lie."

His future father-in-law didn't look at him, but nodded his head. He reached for the glass and took a large gulp.

"Then what are you doing here sulking? You should be sobering up to be ready for the wedding tomorrow." Daniel stepped over a pair of dirty socks and walked around the sofa to stare down at him. "Damn it! What's the matter with you? Your daughter needs you!"

George scoffed and lifted his lids for a moment, but dropped them again quickly, as if he couldn't look Daniel in the eye. "She doesn't need me. Not after the things I said to her."

"That's not true. Every girl needs her father to walk her down the aisle, no matter what happened before."

George shook his head. "I called her a call girl! Don't you get that? I can't take that back. All the apologies in this world won't be enough to restore my relationship to my daughter." He sniffed, and Daniel noticed how the older man's eyes grew moist with tears. "I've screwed up. I should have trusted her. I should have known! She's my little girl. She would have never done anything like that. Why didn't I believe her? Why didn't I take her word for it?"

Daniel lowered himself and moved the newspaper aside to make space on the couch, before sitting down next to him. "We all make mistakes. That's what apologies are for."

"I've made one too many mistakes. She deserves better than me."

"You're still her father. She loves you. Are you really going to ruin your only daughter's wedding day by staying away from it? By letting some stranger walk her down the aisle? Do you know how that will make her feel?" He paused for a moment. "She'll feel abandoned by her father. She'll think you don't love her anymore."

George jumped up. "That's not true! I love her!"

Daniel got up too, jabbing his finger in George's chest. "Then show it! Don't wallow in your own sorrow!" He pointed to the bottle. "Do you think alcohol will resolve the rift between you two? I can tell you it won't! The only way you can fix this is by going to Sabrina and apologizing to her. She'll forgive you. I promise you. Your daughter has the most amazing capacity for forgiveness, and I know that for a fact. In the past, I've hurt her worse than you did. But she forgave me. And it's taught me a lot about your daughter. It's taught me who she is and who I am. And who I would be without her. That's why no matter what happens, I will always ask for her forgiveness, and I will always do whatever is in my power to make her happy. Because the thought of seeing Sabrina unhappy breaks my heart into a million pieces. So, if you love her only a fraction of how I love her, then you will be at that wedding, or I promise you, you'll regret for the rest of your life that you weren't part of the happiest day in your daughter's life."

Without waiting for George's reply, Daniel turned on his heels and walked to the door.

When he turned the handle, George's voice reached him. "What if she doesn't forgive me?"

"That's the risk you'll have to take."

He opened the door and left the room. Now it was up to George to find it in himself to ask for forgiveness. There was nothing else Daniel could do.

27

Daniel glanced at Sabrina as she laughed at something his mother said to her. They were just getting up from the dinner table, where they'd enjoyed the rehearsal dinner, which was taking place in the same tent where the wedding would take place the next day. Sabrina looked beautiful in a simple, yet elegant empire waist evening dress in a soft pastel green that accentuated her breasts as well as her eyes. His eyes drifted lower to where the material flowed over her still-flat stomach. Soon everybody would be able to see that their child was growing inside her. He couldn't suppress the pride and happiness he felt at the thought of Sabrina giving him a child.

"Daniel? Did you hear me?" Paul Gilbert nudged him in the side.

Daniel forced his gaze away from Sabrina. "I'm sorry. What did you say?"

Paul laughed. "I said it's not too late to change your mind. You can pack a bag and we can bust you out of here."

Jay, who'd sidled up to him, nodded in agreement. "Absolutely."

Daniel rolled his eyes at his two friends. "And let me guess, both of you will be more than willing to comfort my jilted fiancée?"

Paul exchanged a grin with Jay. "Somebody will have to."

"Thanks for the offer, but there is nothing in this world that'll keep me from marrying Sabrina tomorrow." He glanced in Sabrina's direction again. "Nothing in the world."

"That's it guys, we've lost him," Paul teased, and everyone around them laughed. "Let's leave this lovesick puppy and get another drink at the bar, before they throw us out. What do you say, Jay?"

"You had me at drink," Jay joked.

Daniel watched the two walk toward the bar and sighed. His eyes wandered over the assembled guests. Tonight only about twenty-five close friends and family members were assembled: his own parents, the members of the Eternal Bachelors Club, Holly and Tim, of course, Sabrina's mother, and several relatives who'd arrived earlier in the day.

However, Sabrina's father had not shown up. Would he be there tomorrow? Daniel hoped so with all his heart, because her father not being there to walk her down the aisle would be the one thing that was still tainting the perfect wedding.

Daniel was about to walk up to Sabrina, when something entered his periphery. He turned his head and stared right at Audrey, who'd walked up to the tent and now entered the lit area. Her red hair glowed like that of a fallen angel seeking revenge. As did her eyes. Audrey was on a mission.

Daniel set his glass of champagne on the nearest table and walked toward her, intent on preventing her from reaching Sabrina and causing any trouble on this otherwise perfect evening.

He stopped in front of her. "You're not welcome here. Leave, or I'll have the police escort you from the property."

"Go ahead, call them! Then I'll tell them that you're blackmailing me!" She shoved a large envelope toward him.

He glanced down at it. "What is this?"

"As if you didn't know!"

Footsteps approached from behind him. Daniel glanced over his shoulder and noticed Tim and Holly hurry in his direction.

"So you got my package," Tim said nonchalantly.

Audrey's glare landed on Tim. "Who the fuck—"

"Oh, I forgot, we've never officially met. I'm Tim, Daniel's best friend. And I look out for him and Sabrina."

Next to him, Holly braced her hands at her hips. "We both do. And we don't like people like you."

"Daniel has nothing to do with this," Tim claimed and gave Daniel a sideways look.

Daniel pointed to the envelope. "The stuff the PI found?"

Tim nodded. "All the gory details." He grinned at Audrey. "Who would have thought that at the tender age of sixteen, our dear Audrey was screwing Kevin Boyd, who, if my calculations are correct, was twenty-seven at the time and already married to Linda."

"I believe it's called statutory rape," Holly added. "Now wouldn't that be a terrible thing if that got out in public and ruined Kevin's life? I suppose your best friend Linda won't take kindly to that revelation. Nor to her husband landing in prison. He'd be a registered sex-offender. What scandal!" She chuckled.

"Do you think this is funny?" Audrey snapped at Holly.

"Almost as funny as you feeding that ridiculous story about Sabrina being a call girl to the paper," Holly retorted.

Audrey scowled and jabbed her index finger in Holly's shoulder. "You bitch!"

Holly shrugged, smiling. "Call me what you must. But frankly, I don't give a flying fuck about your opinion." Then her smile vanished. "Now take your scrawny ass out of here! And if we ever hear a peep out of you again, a copy of these documents will go straight to the district attorney, and we'll be taking Kevin Boyd down and drag you into the mud with him. See how you'll like it then."

Audrey's facial expression changed. She knew she'd lost. With an angry huff, she turned and rushed into the dark.

Daniel turned to Holly and Tim, shaking his head at Tim. "I thought I told you that I didn't need any revenge anymore. My best revenge is being happy with Sabrina."

Tim grinned. "I know that. But I figured a little insurance policy for your happy future without any interference from Audrey ever again was in order. Though eventually she'll figure out that the statute of limitations has already run out on the rape case, it won't change anything about how Kevin's wife or the community will react."

Daniel gripped Tim's shoulder and squeezed it, then hugged Holly. "Thank you, guys."

"Hey, what's going on?" Sabrina's voice drifted to him as she approached.

Daniel released Holly and opened his arms to draw Sabrina against his body. "Holly and Tim just made sure that there will be no more bumps in the road."

Sabrina chuckled and glanced at their two friends. "Why do I get the feeling that this has something to do with Audrey?"

"Because you're a smart woman. I'll tell you all about it later," Daniel answered and kissed her.

28

Sabrina stood staring into the full length mirror, looking at her reflection, and could barely believe that she was the woman in the beautiful white bridal gown. She'd dreamed of this day for as long as she could remember, and now it had finally arrived.

"Oh, Sabrina, you look absolutely breathtaking."

She turned to look at her mother. "Thank you."

Holly and Raffaela walked in a moment later.

"Sabrina, dear, you are so beautiful." Raffaela hugged her gingerly, careful not to crease her dress.

"Thank you." Sabrina sniffed and drew a shaky breath.

"Don't you dare cry," Holly warned. "You'll ruin your makeup and we don't have time to fix it."

Laughing, Sabrina said, "Don't worry. I'll save the tears for the ceremony."

"Good," Raffaela said. "I have something I'd like to give you." She held out a rectangular black velvet box.

Sabrina opened it. Her eyes widened as she perceived the beautiful antique necklace with the brilliant emerald in its center. She looked up at Raffaela. "It's beautiful."

"The stone used to belong to Daniel's grandmother." Raffaela smiled. "Something old."

Tears welled up in Sabrina's eyes. She fanned her face with her hand in the hope of keeping them at bay. "Will you help me put it on?"

"Of course." Raffaela took the necklace out of the box, draped it around Sabrina's neck, and fastened the clasp. "There."

Sabrina reached up and fingered the necklace, then looked into the mirror. The green stone emphasized the green color of her eyes.

"My turn," Holly said excitedly. "Here's your *something borrowed*." Holly opened her palm. "My tear drop diamond earrings that you love so much."

Sabrina looked at them. "Are you sure?"

Holly laughed. "Borrowed, remember?"

Sabrina nodded and hugged Holly, then took the earrings and put them on.

"And finally, your *something blue* and *something new*," her mother said. "You might already have one, so if you do, take it off and use this one instead."

Laughing, Sabrina took the small, gold gift bag and peeked inside. It was a blue silk garter belt.

"Oh, Mom, thanks!" She sensed a blush creeping up her cheeks. "I actually didn't have one. I don't know how I could have forgotten that."

"Well, you have one now. That's all that matters." Her mother smiled while Sabrina slid the garter belt up her thigh.

Sabrina turned back toward the mirror and spun around in front of it for what felt like the hundredth time. Today was the day she would marry the man of her dreams, the man who had made all of her dreams come true. Today she would walk down that aisle and become Daniel's wife.

At the thought of walking down the aisle, her smile faded. Daniel's father had offered to do the honors. She appreciated his offer, but it wouldn't be the same as her own father being there.

She felt a hand on her forearm and looked up. Her mother met her gaze in the mirror. "He'll come, honey."

Sabrina nodded, though she didn't believe it. He wouldn't come. "I guess we'd better ask James to come in now. It's time." She loved Daniel's father. He would be by her side to give her to his son. It would have to do.

Raffaela nodded and walked to the door, when there was a hesitant knock. She opened the door. "Oh!"

Sabrina turned at her surprised gasp. Her breath caught in her throat as she saw the man who stood in the door frame, dressed in a dark suit, a white shirt and a tie. She'd never seen him dressed so handsomely.

"Dad," she whispered, her eyes growing moist with tears once more. Was she dreaming?

His gaze locked with hers as he stepped into the room, setting one hesitant foot in front of the other.

"Holly." Raffaela gestured to Holly and the two of them left the room, easing the door shut behind them, leaving Sabrina alone with her parents.

"I'm so sorry, sweetheart," her father started. "I should have believed you."

Sabrina sniffed. "Oh, Daddy, you're here now. That's all that matters." She opened her arms, and her father took the last few steps that separated them and hugged her.

"Forgive me."

She couldn't say anything, because she was choking up. So she nodded instead and fought against the tears. When he released her from his embrace, he looked her up and down.

"You're so beautiful. I couldn't be prouder of you."

Sabrina smiled and noticed her mother come closer and put a hand on her ex-husband's forearm. He turned to look at her.

"You're a good father, George. You've always been. The two of us were just never meant for each other. But we did one good thing together, didn't we?" Her mother glanced at Sabrina, a wet sheen covering her eyes.

Her father nodded. "Yes, we raised a wonderful daughter." Then he put his arm around his ex-wife and hugged her to him for a brief moment.

It was the most tender gesture she'd ever seen her parents exchange.

"It's time for you to get married." Her father held out his arm to her. "Ready?"

"Yes," she said, taking his proffered arm and allowing him to lead her out of the room, her mother following them.

After walking down the staircase and through the hallway, they reached the porch that led to the tent in the back of the Sinclair's garden. Sabrina felt her heart beat excitedly. Everything was perfect now.

She felt all eyes on her when she and her father stepped onto the carpet that led to the podium on which Daniel and the priest waited, Tim and Holly by their sides. Sabrina's eyes saw only Daniel. He stood at the altar, smiling, his eyes sparkling, looking like Adonis in his tailored tuxedo.

She felt as if walking on a cloud as her father escorted her down the aisle, toward her waiting groom.

When they reached the podium, her father kissed her on the cheek. "I'm so proud of you." Then he stepped aside and took a seat in the first row next to her soon-to-be in-laws.

Daniel took her hand. "You are so beautiful, baby. You steal my breath away."

She couldn't say a word for fear she would cry, because she was so moved.

Father Vincent took a deep breath and began. "We are gathered here today to join together Sabrina Palmer and Daniel Sinclair in holy matrimony. The bride and groom have informed me that they've written their own vows."

Father Vincent nodded at Daniel, signaling for him to start.

Daniel took both of her hands into his and smiled. "Sabrina, my love, you came into my life when I least expected and most needed it. In the short time we've known each other, you have given me more to live for than anyone I've ever met. You're the reason I want to get up in the mornings and the reason I can't wait to go to bed at night."

Sabrina felt her face flush as the crowd chuckled.

Daniel continued undeterred. "Because of you, I'm a better person." He turned to Tim and reached for the ring his friend held out to him. Slowly, deliberately he slid it onto her finger. "I promise to spend every moment for the rest of my life loving you. I promise to make you smile every day, to tell you I love you every night, and to never take you for granted. For as long as I live, I will love and cherish you."

Sabrina's face was wet with tears and her lips trembled. Her hands shook and Daniel gave them a reassuring squeeze.

"Sabrina?" Father Vincent prompted her.

She nodded and wiped her face with the back of her hand. Taking a deep breath, she tried to speak, but her voice failed her. She cleared her throat and tried again.

"Daniel." Her voice was shaky. "Every little girl dreams of finding her knight in shining armor. For so many years I truly believed I would never find him, but then I met you."

She paused and licked her lips, hoping to stave off another round of tears. "You showed me what true love is. Daniel, I fell in love with you the moment I met you without knowing why. But now I know. Because you've proven to me time and again that you'll fight for our happiness and slay every dragon for me. Just when I think I can't possibly love you more, my love for you grows stronger." A sob escaped as she took the ring from Holly and slipped it onto Daniel's finger. "I promise to love you, cherish you, and honor you for as long as I live and fight for our love as much as you do."

Father Vincent raised his hands and announced, "I now pronounce you husband and wife. You may kiss the bride."

Before the last word had left the priest's lips, Daniel's mouth was already capturing Sabrina's for a deep kiss. His lips were soft and gentle, his tongue delicious and imploring. Sabrina slid her hand to his nape and savored their connection. Daniel snaked his arms around her, pulling her flush against him, before releasing her lips for a moment.

"I love you, Mrs. Sabrina Sinclair," he whispered, and then kissed her again.

His kiss left her dizzy, and had he not held her so tightly, she might have fallen. When they turned to their guests, smiling faces greeted them.

They were finally united. Husband and wife.

29

Daniel twirled Sabrina around on the dance floor. The wedding reception, surrounded by happy family and friends, had been perfect. As it drew to a close and the sun had set, making way for a glittering night sky, Daniel couldn't wait to spend the night with his new bride. He'd been thinking about peeling her out of her beautiful wedding dress the moment he'd seen her walking toward him on her father's arm.

"Today has been an absolute dream," Sabrina said with a smile.

"Perfect," he murmured into her ear. "But it's not over yet."

She laughed softly. "Well, I hope not."

"What do you say? Shall we get out of here? I have a car waiting for us to take us to a hotel for the night."

Sabrina looked around. "We still have guests. We can't leave yet."

"It's our wedding. We can do whatever we want. Besides, they all expect us to leave." He motioned to the guests who were dancing, talking, and drinking.

"To a hotel, you said, hmm?"

"Yes. Tonight, we're staying at a hotel. I thought it was more appropriate than staying in my old room in my parents' house. And tomorrow we'll leave for our honeymoon."

Sabrina laced her hands behind his neck. "So, where did you say you're taking me?"

Daniel threw his head back and laughed. "I didn't say."

"You're not going to, are you?"

He shook his head. "Just one clue. It's the most beautiful end of the world."

She brushed her lips over his cheek. "Take me to bed then."

"I thought you'd never ask."

A short while later, a limousine dropped them off at a tucked-away bed and breakfast in Amagansett. A bottle of champagne was waiting for them in their luxurious room, but Daniel wasn't thirsty. All he wanted now was to make love to Sabrina and consummate their marriage.

He crooked his finger to beckon her to come to him.

With catlike grace she approached, the full skirt and sewn-in petticoat of her wedding gown rustling in the quiet of the room. He feasted his eyes on her, on the low neckline of her form-fitted bustier that pushed her breasts up so they looked even fuller than normal, and on her slim waist that made her look like a fairytale princess.

Their eyes met, and he realized she had run her eyes over him in the same fashion.

His hand reached up to caress her cheek and run his fingers along her neck. Her skin was heated. He dipped his head and took her lips, kissing her softly, gently, worshipping her. Seconds passed and turned into minutes as his kiss deepened and became more urgent, more demanding.

Slowly, without saying a word, he began to undress her. He was grateful that she'd chosen a wedding dress with a zipper in the back and not one that had dozens of tiny, round buttons running along her spine like he'd seen on other dresses. At least this way he could guarantee that her dress would remain in one piece and not be ripped by his impatient hands.

Daniel pushed the dress down over her torso, then her hips, until it pooled at her feet. Sabrina stepped out of it, never severing her lips from his. He drew her back against him, feeling her naked skin. She now only wore a strapless bra, panties, and her two-inch heels.

When his hands slid down to her behind, a moan burst from Sabrina's lips and bounced against his.

Her fingers clawed at his tuxedo jacket now, yanking it off his shoulders. Then they worked on his shirt, tugging and pulling at it until she managed to draw it from his waistband. She frantically worked at the buttons, undoing each one quickly and deftly, while he undid his bow tie and tossed it to the floor.

The feel of her hands and fingers roaming his chest when she pushed the shirt off him had him trembling with anticipation. Then her hands reached lower and slid over the zipper of his black pants. He ripped his lips from hers and gasped for air. Then she squeezed him through the fabric.

"Fuck!" he ground out.

"A little sensitive?" his hot little seductress murmured.

He met her teasing gaze. "Don't play with fire if you can't stand the heat."

Daniel scooped her up into his arms and carried her to the bed, where he laid her on top of the turned-down sheets. Then he divested himself of his shoes, socks, and took off his pants and boxer briefs. Finally he felt like he could breathe again.

When he looked at her, she noticed that her gaze had dropped to his cock that curved upward, hard and heavy. Ready for her. She licked her lips as if she wanted to taste him, but tonight she wouldn't get a chance to do that to him. He would lose control if he allowed her to wrap her hot little mouth around his cock, and come so quickly that it would all be over in a flash.

"God, you're so beautiful." He bent over her and slid his hands underneath her panties. She lifted herself off the mattress so he could slide them down her slender legs. When he reached her feet, he pulled her G-string over her high-heeled, white sandals.

"Take your bra off," he demanded, his voice getting huskier with every second.

He watched in fascination as she reached behind her and opened the clasp, then freed her breasts from their cage. The garment landed on the floor.

Sabrina looked sexier and more seductive than he'd ever seen her. He glanced at her sandals again. Yes, he'd let her keep those. It reminded him of the time they'd made love on her ex-boss's desk, right after they'd signed that ridiculous contract that made her his exclusive escort.

Slowly, he slid over her, bracing himself on his elbows and knees, her thighs parting automatically to make space for him.

His mouth found hers again, and he kissed her deeply, passionately, longingly, while his hands caressed her silken skin. Beneath his fingers he felt her tremble.

A sigh came from her lips when he came up for air.

"Daniel . . . "

Hearing her say his name like this—whispery, needy, seductive—shot a spear of desire through his core and right into his balls, pulling them up tightly below the base of his rock-hard cock. When he pressed his hips against her pelvis, the warmth of her body rippled through him, igniting a fire in his body that only she could extinguish.

"Sabrina, my love," he murmured as he descended into her warm and welcoming body. Inch by agonizing inch, he slid deeper until he was seated to the hilt.

Her legs wrapped around him, holding him close to her. He felt the length of her heels press against his butt, sending another bolt of electricity through him.

"Yes." Sabrina's hands dug into his shoulders, pulling him down to her for another kiss.

He had no objections and took her mouth like an invading barbarian, like a conqueror intent on taking the prize that was offered to him. He'd never felt so primal, so raw. Finally Sabrina was his. Nothing could ever come between them again. They had overcome all obstacles, all hurdles that had been placed in their path.

Her tight pussy clamped around him, pulling his cock deeper into her, squeezing him harder. Daniel steadily and skillfully plunged in and out of her, driving himself to the edge of insanity, then retreating again to buy himself more time until the inevitable would happen. But with each sequence, it became harder to control his body, more difficult to hold back the need for release. Being with Sabrina was always like this: intense, all-consuming, and fiery. She aroused him more than any other woman ever had.

A thin sheen of sweat had built on their bodies and every time they slapped together, the sound of their lovemaking reverberated in the room. Together with their uncontrolled breaths, their sighs and moans, it sounded like a symphony of lust and passion. It was a song he didn't want to end, though he knew he couldn't hold on much longer.

From the way Sabrina's chest heaved and her hips grinded against him, he knew she was as close as he. There was no holding it back now.

"*Per sempre.*" Forever, he thought as he withdrew only to plunge back into her.

A visible shudder raced through her body and crashed into him just as his cock exploded inside her, pumping his seed into her.

While her body still trembled from the aftereffects of her orgasm, as did his, Sabrina's lips moved.

"*Per sempre*," she repeated and locked eyes with his.

It was a promise he'd hold her to.

EPILOGUE

Holly looked at Paul, who stood at the bar at the end of the tent, waiting for the bartender to mix him another drink. While she'd been introduced to him during the rehearsal dinner, she'd barely spoken more than ten words to him. It was something she wanted to change. And not only because Sabrina had told her to be nice to him. No, to a man like him she wanted to talk anytime. And not just talk. She wanted a lot more.

She ran her eyes over him. His tuxedo fit him like a second skin, and he had the kind of suave James-Bond-look about him that she'd thought only James Bond or Cary Grant could carry off without looking smarmy. She knew exactly how a man like Paul would be in bed. She knew how he would undress her, how he would touch her, how his body would grind against her. How his cock would slide into her with one forceful thrust and touch her womb, fill her, stretch her.

She knew all that just by looking at him. She always avoided men like him. She preferred her clients to be average in bed. It made it easier to remain detached and keep her emotions out of the game. That's why she avoided men like Paul. Because for once she might actually feel something.

As her feet carried her closer to him, even though her brain told her to stay away from him, she started justifying the action she was about to take. She was on vacation. Wasn't everybody allowed a vacation fling? A one-night-stand that would lead to nothing or to everything? Even an escort had to forget her work occasionally and let herself go and only do what her heart told her.

Besides, hadn't she already decided to quit the escort business, even though she hadn't told her boss Misty yet? Hadn't she already made up her mind that she was done with all this? So what was the harm in flirting with a man like Paul? What was the harm of letting him know that she was available tonight if he wanted to take her to his bed?

Before she could truly answer her own questions, she'd already reached him. He must have seen her from the corner of his eye, because he turned and smiled at her, while his eyes dropped down to the neckline of her red bridesmaid's dress. When she noticed his admiring gaze, she silently thanked Sabrina for not sticking her into something pink or orange. Red worked so much better on her.

"Holly," Paul greeted her, lifting his gaze back to her eyes. "So it's almost over." He motioned to where some of the guests gathered their things and started to leave.

She lowered her eyelids halfway, but never avoided his gaze. "It doesn't have to be."

Paul's chest suddenly lifted as if he were pulling in a deep breath. "No, it doesn't have to." He set down the glass the bartender had handed him and reached for her hand instead. "I don't believe we've danced yet."

When he drew her into his arms and maneuvered her toward the dance floor, Holly's heart began to beat excitedly. His touch was electrifying! With one hand he clasped hers, with the other he pressed against the small of her back to pull her toward his body. She could feel the heat radiate from him despite the evening breeze coming from the ocean.

As he led her into the first turn of a slow foxtrot, she searched for something to say to cover her nervousness. This wasn't like her. She wasn't nervous and shy when it came to men. So why did she feel compelled to bridge the silence between them? "Sabrina said you saved her from the woman in the lingerie store."

"That was nothing," Paul claimed, smiling.

"It meant a lot to Sabrina. You were there for her when she needed somebody. She's my best friend. You were nice to her. That means I'll be nice to you." Her pulse raced as she said words she knew he could only interpret one way.

Paul dipped his head to her ear. His hot breath sent a shiver racing down her body. "How nice?"

"Very nice for as long as you want to, anywhere you want to." Her breath hitched at her own daring words. She'd just lost her mind and offered a man she barely knew a night without limits.

"Then what are we still doing on the dance floor?" he answered and slid his hand onto her backside, pressing his groin against her. Already, she could feel a hard muscle there, one that would only grow harder and larger as the night progressed, she hoped.

Feeling his arousal gave her newfound confidence. "Shouldn't we at least finish this one dance so people don't stare at us, when we're rushing out of here?"

"Holly, Holly," he murmured and pressed a hot kiss below her ear. "We can finish this dance if you insist, but I'll guarantee you that if we do that, people will start staring at us. Your choice."

When she felt his pelvis rub against her again, she knew there was really no choice.

"I've never cared much for dancing anyway."

"Wise choice," he answered and released her from his embrace only to take her hand and lead her to the exit of the tent.

She didn't care where he took her as long as something soft would cushion her back and something hard would thrust inside her.

THE END

ABOUT THE AUTHOR

Tina Folsom was born in Germany and has been living in English speaking countries for over 20 years, the last 12 of them in San Francisco, where she's married to an American.

Tina has always been a bit of a globe trotter: after living in Lausanne, Switzerland, she briefly worked on a cruise ship in the Mediterranean, then lived a year in Munich, before moving to London. There, she became an accountant. But after 8 years she decided to move overseas.

In New York she studied drama at the American Academy of Dramatic Arts, then moved to Los Angeles a year later to pursue studies in screenwriting. This is also where she met her husband, who she followed to San Francisco three months after first meeting him.

In San Francisco, Tina worked as a tax accountant and even opened her own firm, then went into real estate, however, she missed writing. In 2008 she wrote her first romance and never looked back.

She's always loved vampires and decided that vampire and paranormal romance was her calling. She now has 18 novels in English and dozens in other languages (Spanish, German, and French) and continues to write, as well as have her existing novels translated.

For more about Tina Folsom:

www.tinawritesromance.com
http://www.facebook.com/TinaFolsomFans
Twitter: @Tina_Folsom
Email: tina@tinawritesromance.com

Made in the USA
Charleston, SC
30 April 2014